"You're a good m... **"You let him kno...** **that he's importa...** **...ot like my father..."**

He hadn't meant to say those last four words, but it was as if they had been ripped from the deepest part of his heart.

"Not like your father? What do you mean, Thorn?" she asked, her face puzzled, her eyes searching the depths of his gaze.

Perhaps it was time to get it out in the open. No wound could heal if it was left to fester.

"My birth cost my mother her health," he told her. "She was never well afterward, and she died before I was old enough to remember her. She'd wanted to name me Thornton, after her father, but after she was gone, my father just called me Thorn. He made sure I knew it was because I was a thorn in his side…"

"Oh, Thorn!" she cried. And suddenly she had thrown her arms around him as she began to cry.

He was so astonished—and moved, because no one had found him worthy of weeping over before—that he could only wrap his arms around her and pull her close…

Laurie Kingery is a Texas transplant to Ohio who writes romance set in post–Civil War Texas. She was nominated for a Carol Award for her second Love Inspired Historical novel, *The Outlaw's Lady*, and is currently writing a series about mail-order grooms in a small town in the Texas Hill Country.

Books by Laurie Kingery

Love Inspired Historical

Hill Country Christmas
The Outlaw's Lady

Bridegroom Brothers

The Preacher's Bride Claim

Brides of Simpson Creek

Mail Order Cowboy
The Doctor Takes a Wife
The Sheriff's Sweetheart
The Rancher's Courtship
The Preacher's Bride
Hill Country Cattleman
A Hero in the Making
Hill Country Courtship
Lawman in Disguise

Visit the Author Profile page at Harlequin.com.

LAURIE KINGERY

Lawman in Disguise

HARLEQUIN® LOVE INSPIRED® HISTORICAL

Recycling programs
for this product may
not exist in your area.

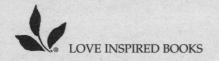 LOVE INSPIRED BOOKS

ISBN-13: 978-0-373-28367-5

Lawman in Disguise

Trust in the Lord with all thine heart; and lean not unto thine own understanding. In all thy ways acknowledge him, and he shall direct thy path.

—*Proverbs* 3:5–6

To Deb Siegenthal and Rhonda Gibson,
the best encouragers anywhere, as well as being
fine novelists themselves, and as always, to Tom

Chapter One

Simpson Creek, Texas
August 1870

He was at the end of his strength, and he supposed this barn behind someone's Simpson Creek house was as good a place to die as anywhere else. At least Ace, his horse, was apt to find some forage before he gave up on his master and wandered off. Thorn only hoped that if the law connected the riderless horse to the outlaws involved in the bank robbery, they wouldn't be able to find him here, or they'd be apt to string him up before he could explain.

Sooner or later, he knew that he'd have to talk to local law enforcement. He'd explain that he was a State Police officer, assigned to infiltrate the infamous Griggs gang and collect enough evidence to bring them to justice for their many crimes. He was prepared for the local sheriff's skepticism. Thorn just hoped it didn't come at the end of a loaded gun. This town had shot him enough already.

Weakened as he was by the loss of blood, his dismount turned into an ungraceful collapse into the aisle between the stalls, observed by no one but a trio of chickens scrabbling along in search of bugs and stray oats. The chickens fluttered and clucked in alarm when he collapsed, and he groaned as the fiery pain of his wound punished him for the violent movement. But once they finished their squawking, they seemed content to leave him be. Ace sidled away uneasily before spotting a mound of hay in the corner with a bucket atop it, and ambling toward it, his injured rider forgotten.

Though his vision was blurry, Thorn could see that he was lying right in front of an open stall. The straw bedding looked far from new, but it would at least be a little softer than the dirt. Smothering more groans, he crawled toward it.

He hoped whoever found his dead body wouldn't be too upset by the discovery. It might have been nice to have a cold sip of water before he breathed his last, but one couldn't have everything... As soon as he reached the dark haven of the middle of the stall, oblivion overtook him and he closed his eyes.

He awakened with a start some time later to the sound of the barn door creaking open and footsteps trudging toward him. How much later it was, Thorn wasn't sure, but the light from the barn door hadn't faded much, so he guessed it to be late afternoon.

"Dumb ol' eggs," he heard a boy's voice mutter. "Why do *I* always hafta be the one to gather 'em?"

Thorn froze. If the boy was hunting eggs, his search might very well bring him into this stall, and he would be discovered. The boy sounded young. Young enough to be scared at the sight of a man badly wounded? Or old enough to be ready and willing to defend his family's barn from intruders? There was no way to tell, which meant the safest thing for Thorn to do would be to hide somewhere out of sight. But there was no time to find another hiding place, and he certainly didn't have the strength to run.

Was his horse still in the barn? He listened, and sure enough, he could hear the beast's teeth grinding away at something at the end of the barn aisle. Maybe Thorn might be able to reach Ace and flee before the boy could set up a hue and cry...

"Hey, fella, where'd you come from?" he heard the boy call out, and Thorn knew that the kid had spotted his horse. "Ma ain't gonna be happy you found her bucket of chicken feed. Let's move you into a stall, and I'll pull that heavy saddle off so's you can rest for a spell while I find out where you come from."

Thorn heard Ace's snort of displeasure as he was pulled away from the source of his snack, the clop of his hooves down the aisle, the creak of a stall door opening on rusty hinges. The kid had chosen another stall, so Thorn was safe for now…but he couldn't count on that safety lasting. Not when the boy was bound to start searching for how Ace had gotten into the barn in the first place. As if responding to his fears, he heard the lad's sudden intake of breath, and his shocked question, "Is that *blood?*"

Thorn's wounds must have leaked blood onto the saddle. Oh no, had he left a trail all over the barn floor, as well? He knew better than to be so careless. If nothing else, being an outlaw for the past few months had taught him how to cover his tracks. But he'd been so exhausted, he hadn't even thought to check to see what kind of trail he was leaving behind.

The door to the stall where Ace had been led slammed shut, and Thorn heard the gelding shift restively. The boy's footsteps quickened and came closer as each stall door was opened and shut. His vision had been fuzzy around the edges when he'd entered the barn, but he thought there'd been only about four stalls…

He wished there'd been enough hay to cover himself with, or something to hide behind, but he doubted that would have worked, anyway. Stifling a groan, he crouched with the intent of grabbing the boy and putting his hand over the kid's mouth until he could convince him to keep quiet—

Then the door of the stall where he lay was yanked open. "Mister! What are you doin' there? Stay where you are, or I'll beat your brains out!" the boy cried with surprising ferocity, given his small size. He had grabbed up a piece of wood that looked as if it had played a role in stickball games, and was swinging it around in a threatening manner, as if he'd be only too glad to make good his threat. He looked to be about twelve or so, Thorn thought, a boy on the cusp of adolescence and feeling the need to prove himself.

"Quiet down, b-boy, I…I won't…won't hurt you, I promise I won't," he muttered, reaching for him, but the boy danced back out of his reach. Thorn knew he wasn't up to clambering to his feet and grabbing the lad, but apparently he looked more dangerous than he actually felt at the moment because the boy kept a wary eye on him, obviously ready to act if the intruder tried anything.

"Won't h-hurt you," Thorn repeated, hoping he sounded convincing. "Don't want to hurt…anybody. Need…help…" His legs wouldn't hold him up any longer and he sank back into the hay, feeling the sweat dripping from his forehead. And the blood still dripping from his shoulder. At least the wound on his leg seemed to have closed up.

"Who are you?" the boy asked, daring to come closer as he stared at the man.

"My name's Thorn," he said. "What's yours?"

The boy's expression was fearful, as if he thought possessing his name would give Thorn some power over him, but evidently he thought it was only fair to supply it, since the man had admitted his own.

"Billy Joe...H-Henderson," he quavered, in a voice on the edge of deepening into manhood. "What happened t' you? Did you get attacked by Injuns?"

Thorn felt his lips curve upward slightly at the question, and Billy Joe looked embarrassed, as if he had already realized his guess was ridiculous. Attacks by Indians certainly happened often enough—in fact, Thorn thought he'd heard tell that this town had had problems with them before—but his injuries certainly didn't fit the profile. If Comanches had attacked, the whole town would have heard the war whoops and the commotion, and there'd be more victims than just this one man. Besides, he didn't have any arrows sticking out of him and he hadn't been scalped...

He saw the boy's face change the moment he realized the truth.

"You're one of them bank robbers, ain't you?" the boy breathed, clearly awed. "You got shot makin' your getaway, right? You're a real live *outlaw*."

Thorn started to shake his head, then stopped and stared at Billy Joe, trying to think what to tell him. He couldn't tell him the truth—that he was working secretly to infiltrate the gang on orders from the State Police. A boy couldn't be expected to keep a secret like that, and Thorn would be in serious danger if his true identity was exposed. But if the boy thought he was an outlaw, surely he'd feel obligated to run to the sheriff, or at least to tell his pa, who would then go to the sheriff himself.

"Don't worry, I won't tell nobody," Billy Joe whispered, crouching low and holding out his hand to the man. "I want to be an outlaw, too, when I grow up, so I won't turn you in. I seen you and all the other outlaws gallopin' away after the holdup—not close-like," he told Thorn quickly, as if he thought Thorn would worry that he could identify all of them. "But my friend Dan was just comin' out of the mercantile with his ma, across from the bank, and he told me all about what he saw. Wait'll I tell him you was hidin' out *in our barn*," he said, obviously feeling honored.

"You just said you wouldn't tell anybody," Thorn pointed out. "I could be in danger if you did."

The boy looked startled. "Oh, I wouldn't tell till after you got away," he hastened to assure him. He still looked nervous, and Thorn realized in that moment how he must look to the boy, with his shirt blood-spattered, his eyes probably wide and wild, and his face pale from the loss of blood. He was certain he looked dangerous, and to a boy that had to seem a lot more exciting than the ranchers and farmers he probably saw every day. Thorn wasn't really surprised that he dreamed of being an outlaw. Boys dreamed of all sorts of foolish things.

"You *are* one of them outlaws, aren't you?" Billy Joe persisted.

Thorn nodded, watching the boy. "Yes, I was with the gang that robbed your bank today."

"Ain't my bank, Mr. Thorn—my ma and me, we don't have so much as a plugged nickel in it. We ain't got enough money to keep any in a bank. So why are you all bloody?" Billy Joe asked.

"I got shot during the robbery," Thorn admitted. "I lost a lot of blood."

"I gotta get you some help," Billy Joe told him. "The doctor—"

"No, you can't bring the doctor here!" Thorn cried in alarm, jerking his hand out, though he knew he couldn't move fast enough to stop Billy Joe if the boy took off—not with his injuries. "He'll bring the law…"

"But I can't just let you die!" Billy Joe insisted.

"Even if it was safe," Thorn tried to explain, "your doc's got work enough to keep him busy in town to-night." He was trying to think of how to explain to the boy that other townspeople had been hurt in the robbery—the bank president and the teller—and that the doctor would be tied up tending to them, when both Thorn and Billy Joe froze at the sound of foot-steps entering the barn and coming toward the stall.

"Billy Joe, where *are* you?" called a female voice. "Didn't I tell you I needed the eggs before I could cook our supper?"

The lad went still, staring wide-eyed at Thorn, and Thorn stared back, equally dismayed. But there was nowhere to hide. The boy's lips silently formed the words *my ma*.

"Billy Joe, who were you talking to?" his mother demanded from just outside the stall. "If one of your no-account friends is here distracting you when you should be doing what I asked, he'll just have to go home. I—"

She pushed open the stall door, then shrieked as she spotted Thorn crouching in the straw. He saw her wrench the stick out of Billy Joe's hand and take a firm hold on it—as if a stick could protect them from a desperate man. She pushed her son behind her, clearly determined to stand between him and danger. He was surprised she didn't yell for her husband. Maybe the man was away from the house, still at work?

"Who're you? And what are you doing talking to my son?" she demanded. "Billy Joe, run and fetch the sheriff!"

But Billy Joe remained rooted to the spot. "Ma, Mr. Thorn—he won't hurt us," he said. "He promised."

It sounded to Thorn as if the boy was making a valiant effort to make his tone sound adult and reassuring, not frantic and whiny like a little kid's.

"He's wounded, that's all. Ma, we gotta help him, we gotta!"

Thorn saw the woman's eyes narrow as she listened to her son, then she aimed that piercing gaze back at him. There was not an ounce of belief in her eyes that he was anything but a low-down polecat.

Smart lady, Thorn thought. *I wouldn't believe that someone like me could be trusted, either, after looking at me.* He braced himself, expecting to see the woman yank her son out of the barn by his collar, if necessary. Shortly after that, the sheriff would appear and the jig would be well and truly up. Thorn had to try to keep that from happening.

He raised both arms, wincing at the effort. He couldn't raise the one that was wounded all the way up. Even just lifting it halfway hurt like blazes. "I really don't mean any harm, Mrs. Henderson, ma'am. I just rode in here looking for..." *A quiet place to die*, he thought, but he didn't want to say that and alarm her further. The idea of a dead body in her barn might cause the lady to swoon—though she didn't precisely look to be the swooning type. She was actually rather pretty, in a quiet, careworn sort of way, or she would be, if she ever got some rest. She had hair of a hue he'd heard called ash blond before, and deep-set, gray-blue eyes that saw right through a man's bluster. But even with the tiredness that etched her face, she had a quiet sort of dignity he respected. He hoped it wouldn't make her madder that he'd used her name. "Peace and quiet..."

"That may be, but your horse has helped himself to an entire bucket of chicken feed," Mrs. Henderson replied tartly, jerking her head toward the other end of the barn. "I certainly hope you have the money to square that with us. I can't afford to buy more feed."

"Sorry, ma'am, I'll pay you for it, soon as I can," Thorn murmured.

The woman made a dismissive gesture, as if she was accustomed to empty promises and had no use for them. "So how did you get injured? The truth now—I'll know if you lie," she said.

"I got shot at the bank when the men I was riding with robbed it," he said, locking her gaze with his while hoping against hope she would read the message in his eyes that there was more to the story than that. Had she noticed the way he'd phrased it, saying that the bank was robbed by the men he was riding with—not by him? "I promise you, I intend no harm to you or your family, nor will I steal anything— beyond what my horse has already taken. I... I just couldn't ride any farther."

Her eyes left his and focused on his bloodstained shirt. "How badly are you wounded?"

"I was hit in the shoulder and the leg, and bled a lot. I think the leg wound may just be a graze. With a little care, though, I'm hoping I won't get lead poisoning," he added, with more confidence than he actually felt. But he hadn't expired yet, so maybe there was reason to hope. "Soon as I'm fit to ride, I'll leave here."

Daisy Henderson heard the unspoken questions within his statement—*would she provide the care he needed to recover, and let him stay hidden here until his wounds were healed?*

"Oh, so you're a gentleman bank robber, is that right, Mr. Thorn?" she retorted, allowing an edge of scorn into her voice. "So you weren't the one who shot the bank president, or the teller?"

"Ma," her son protested, clearly embarrassed that she was questioning his new hero. "He told me he didn't want to hurt nobody. I think we should take him at his word."

She rounded on the boy. "Billy Joe Henderson, I'll thank you not to question your mother when I'm doing what I must to keep us safe," she said. She wasn't at all happy about the admiring tone in his voice in regard to the wounded man at their feet, and the way her son seemed to want to protect an *outlaw*.

"But, Ma…" Flushed and crestfallen, the boy stared at the hay under his boots.

A glance at the wounded man showed traces of discomfort in his eyes as his gaze shifted from her to her son.

"Billy Joe, mind your mother," he said gently. "She only wants what's good for you, and she has no reason to believe that I'm no danger to either one of you." He turned back to Daisy. "And no, I wasn't the one who shot the bank president or the teller. I was as surprised as the ones who got shot when the lead started flying. Griggs—that's the leader of the gang—had said there was to be no shooting unless it became necessary. And it wasn't necessary from my point of view—none of the bank employees had offered any resistance. The gang shot them purely for their amusement, far as I could tell," Thorn said.

"If no one in the bank was putting up any resistance or trying to fight, then how did you get shot?" she asked, perplexed by his story. He talked about the gang as if he wasn't one of them himself. But he must have been right in the thick of the robbery to have gotten shot.

"As we turned to leave the bank, I heard a bang and it felt like someone had punched me, and then there was this stinging in my shoulder. I looked around, and saw that the bank president was suddenly holding a revolver, of all things, aimed at me. And that was funny, really, since I'd put myself in range by trying to stop Zeke—Zeke Tomlinson, he's one of the Griggs gang and the one who first started firing off his gun—from shooting anyone else. Then another member of the gang—Bob Pritchard—shot the bank president in the shoulder in retaliation, just as he was aiming to fire again. That's the shot that grazed my leg. And then it was time for us to skedaddle."

"No one's looked at those injuries since then?"

"That's why I wanted to go fetch the doctor for him, Ma," Billy Joe interjected.

"As I was about to tell your son when you came in, ma'am, I figure your town doctor is pretty busy right now, just tending the bank president and the teller. He doesn't need another patient."

Daisy ignored that comment for now. "Billy Joe, go back into the house and stay there—right now," she said firmly, when the boy seemed loath to leave. "You're to keep out of the barn until I decide what's to be done."

Billy Joe's lower lip jutted out rebelliously, but after uttering a big sigh, he trudged out of the barn, much to Daisy's relief. She sighed herself and looked after her son for a moment before turning back to Thorn.

"I don't know what I'm going to do with him," she murmured. "He's been through a lot in the past couple of years…and I don't want you being here to disrupt our family after everything that's happened already."

Thorn looked puzzled. "Ma'am, I promise you that I'm no threat to your family, but if you think your husband would object to me staying here in your barn till I'm able to travel, I can move on." Left unspoken was the fact that he also wanted her to avoid telling the sheriff his whereabouts. She saw that he was watching carefully for her reaction. "If you wouldn't mind, I'd prefer to wait to move till nightfall, though…"

She'd hoped he wouldn't guess her family's situation, but he was too clever. "I… I probably shouldn't tell you this," she said, avoiding his eyes, "but I won't lie. I'm a widow…have been for a couple of years now," she added, when his gaze dropped to her clothes, which were shabby and threadbare, but definitely not the black of recent mourning. "Billy Joe is my only child, and there's no one living here but the two of us. I don't even have any kin still living. So there's no one else to object to your presence. And that's why I said Billy Joe had been through a lot lately…"

I should have said, "We've been through a lot lately," she realized as soon as she had spoken. It sounded as if she didn't miss her husband much, which was a horrible thing to admit to a stranger, even though it was true.

"I'm sorry for your loss," the wounded man said automatically. "And for how it's affected your son. I'd guess that without a father around to set him straight, you're not happy to hear your boy talking like an outlaw was someone to look up to," he concluded for her.

"No, I'm not," she agreed, and thought he saw too much with those dark, knowing eyes. She met his gaze with her chin upturned, daring him to criticize her parenting. He certainly wouldn't be the first to think she couldn't raise her son properly as a single mother. There were plenty of good people in Simpson Creek, as she knew firsthand. But there were plenty of mean-spirited gossips, too.

"And I can understand that," he told her, looking as if he wanted to say more about why he understood. "Mrs. Henderson, I can't tell you the whole truth about my situation—for the sake of yours and the boy's safety and my own—but I can tell you I'm *not* an outlaw, and that I have an honest and honorable reason for riding with the gang. And I promise, you and your son have absolutely nothing to fear from me. If you'd be willing to let me hide here, I'll leave as soon as I can after that, and you can forget you ever laid eyes on me."

Should she take him at his word or not? Why should she take a chance that he was telling her the truth?

There was sincerity shining in his dark eyes, but she'd learned from bitter experience that sincerity could be faked. William Henderson, Billy Joe's father, had been a sweet-talking man with a sincere expression on his face when they'd courted, but shortly after they'd wed, he had turned her life into a nightmare that had lasted until he'd been taken away to prison.

"Again," Thorn continued, "I know you have no reason to believe what I'm about to tell you, but I'll say it, anyway—I'm a Christian, law-abiding man, Mrs. Henderson. The Bible is my guide."

William had said he was a Christian man, too, but he'd twisted the Scriptures to excuse his cruelty to her till she'd almost stopped believing there was a God who cared what happened to her and her little boy. It wasn't until her husband was killed in a prison riot that she felt able to take an easy breath and start to believe in God's care for her again.

"Then why are you—" she began, then caught herself. "Never mind—you said you couldn't say, so I won't press you to give me an answer you can't give. I'll just say that I'm a Christian woman, too."

At least she tried to be, even though it was hard. Was it truly Christian of her to distrust Thorn—to distrust nearly every man she encountered—because of her abusive late husband? Forgiveness was something she struggled with. She knew it was her duty as a Christian, but it was so very hard to find forgiveness in her heart for the man who had beaten her and Billy Joe for all those years.

Had the Lord sent Thorn to her as a test, to see if she could show compassion and understanding to a man who, by all appearances, was a criminal like her husband? Maybe. The Bible said the Lord worked in mysterious ways—certainly they'd never been clear to her. But that didn't stop her from wanting to bring herself, and especially her son, closer to God—to live within His plan for their lives.

"We go to church every other Sunday," she informed Thorn, "which is all I can get off from work, whether Billy Joe's wanting to attend or not. And I try to get him to go without me when I'm working. I'm trying to be the best ma I can to him. I'm hoping if I 'train my child up in the way he should go,' as the Bible says, he'll turn out to be a better man than his father was." And what of the example she herself set for her son? Could she teach him a lesson in Christian compassion by letting Thorn stay with them?

The man in question was now staring at her, and she guessed he was wondering if she was always so forthright with strangers. But she had always used that very plain speaking as a sort of armor against the world.

"I have an idea," he began with some hesitation, "if you're going to let me stay, that is. You might use that permission to motivate your son, since he wants you to help me. Tell him I can only stay if he does whatever you say, whatever he's been reluctant to do…such as finishing his chores, going to church, minding his manners and suchlike. But that's up to you, ma'am, of course—you know your son best, and I hope you don't mind the suggestion."

She blinked in surprise, then considered what he'd said. "You know, that's actually a good idea," she murmured after a moment. She could use this to teach her son about being a Christian, *and* give him a reason to behave, all in one. "Very well, Mr. Thorn…you may stay—for now."

"Much obliged, ma'am. I won't give you cause to regret it."

But could he really promise that? Even if she believed him, that he was riding with the outlaws for an honorable reason, he was still technically on the run from the law. If her neighbors found out she was harboring a fugitive, she'd never survive the scandal…

She asked another question to distract herself from that worry. "Umm, you didn't say, exactly—is Thorn your first or your last name?"

"First name," he said, and his face twisted as if the name caused him to feel bitter. "Last name is Dawson."

He must have seen the skeptical look on her face. "I'm telling you the truth, Mrs. Henderson."

"All right then," she said. "You can stay here until you're well enough to ride off, Mr. Dawson. But I can't have you dying on me. Having a dead outlaw's body in my barn would be a little hard to explain. Simpson Creek has a very good doctor, and I insist on having him see you. I have no nursing experience, so I need his guidance on how to treat you, if you're to recover. You can tell him the same thing you told me," she added quickly, guessing he was about to protest. And that made her irritable. She was trying to help him, and he wanted to question that?

"And you needn't look so doubtful," she snapped. "Dr. Walker isn't your usual small-town quacksalver. He knows all the latest things in medicine, and I've seen him save folks who were at death's door. He doesn't use all those snake oil remedies like calomel, either."

"All right, all right," the wounded man said, waving a hand in surrender. "Have him come—if he's not needed treating the others in town."

She saw him wince and guessed that the movement sent fresh, stabbing waves of pain lancing through his wounded shoulder. Either that, or he felt guilty at the thought of the bank president and teller who had been shot.

"I'll send Billy Joe for him," she said. "And don't worry, I'll tell him to go straight to the doctor's house, and not to breathe a word of your presence here to any of his no-account friends." She could easily picture Billy Joe, flushed with triumph at having a "real gen-u-ine outlaw" in his barn, bragging to all his pals. As Daisy turned to leave the stall, she said a little prayer that her son would be obedient enough to follow her command. She still didn't know whether or not to believe the man who lay in the stall when he said he wasn't an outlaw, but just this once, she'd take on faith something she'd been told. She just hoped she wouldn't come to regret trusting him in her and Billy Joe's lives.

And if he wasn't an outlaw, what was he doing riding with them?

Chapter Two

Daisy sighed as Billy Joe took off down the street at a run toward Dr. Walker's house at the other end of Simpson Creek, leaving the kitchen door gaping open behind him, as usual. Out of habit, she went and shut it, but her mind wasn't on the flies she was trying to keep out, or her son's surprisingly quick agreement to her conditions for letting the wounded man stay. It was fixed on Thorn himself.

Thorn—odd first name; short for something else, like Thornton?—Dawson was a puzzle to her. She'd told him so much about herself, but had learned so little about him in return. All she really knew was that he was hurt—and that she'd promised to help.

And that meant she shouldn't be just sitting here, gazing out the window at the barn and wondering about the man lying in one of the stalls. She should be getting bandaging materials ready—or would Doc

Walker bring them? At the very least, she could put a pot of water on to boil in case the doctor needed it.

By the time she'd gathered an old sheet and set some water to boil on the stove, though, Billy Joe still hadn't returned with the doctor. Her stomach rumbled, reminding her that it was getting late and she still hadn't done anything about supper. She was sorely tempted to go out to the barn to gather the eggs that her son hadn't collected, but to do so would mean being alone with the stranger out there. Yes, they were alone in the barn before, when she'd sent Billy Joe away, but in that moment protecting her son had been her top—her only—priority. But Billy Joe was fine now, and there was no reason for her to pass any more time than necessary with a strange man. She'd have to face him again at some point, of course, since he'd be staying with them for who knew how long, but it wasn't something she was ready to do again just yet.

Minutes later, Daisy nearly jumped out of her skin when she saw the shadow of a man's figure ripple into the yard between the house and the barn. There hadn't been many full-grown men on her property since her husband had been taken away to jail—and she still felt the familiar sense of dread at the sight of a man's shadow. But it was the doctor, finally, carrying his big black leather bag. Billy Joe ran before him, looking back over his shoulder with an obvious impatience for the physician to reach the wounded man. She'd better go out and see what assistance Dr. Walker might require from her. Would he think she was a foolish woman for calling the doctor first before the sheriff, under the circumstances?

By the time she got out to the barn, Dr. Walker had already hung his frock coat over the half door of the stall and rolled up his sleeves, and was peering at Dawson's shoulder wound. The doctor had already pulled away what remained of the bloody shirt off the outlaw's shoulder.

"Thanks for coming, Dr. Walker," Daisy murmured, feeling her stomach roil as she flinched away from the sight of the dried streaks of blood, as well as the man's bare, well-muscled shoulder. She never dealt well with the sight of blood—not since she was a girl, and Peter…but no, she wouldn't think of her brother now. That was a memory best left buried.

"Mmm. I'd have been here sooner, but I was a mite busy with Mr. Amos and his bank teller. I'm sure you'll be glad to hear that they'll live, by all indications," he muttered.

"*I'm* real glad to hear it," Thorn said, and he sounded like he meant it. "It was a lowdown, cowardly thing, what Zeke did, firing like that when there was no cause for it at all. If I'd noticed him aiming just a minute sooner, maybe I could've…" He shook his head. "Makes no difference what I would or *could've* done—I know that. There's no changing what happened. But I sure am mighty glad to hear that both of those men will be all right."

Dr. Walker gave him a nod of acknowledgment. "You'll recover, too, once I get the bullet out of your shoulder. But you must know, you've lost a lot of blood…"

She was aware that her son was staring at the shoulder wound with a fascinated horror. "Billy Joe, go inside the house."

"But I'm gonna help the doctor!" Billy Joe protested. "He said he'd need someone to hold the lantern so he could see to clean and dress the wounds."

She was sure a clear view of Thorn's injuries was not a sight that a young boy should be seeing. "I'll do that," she said in a tone that brooked no disobedience. She would simply have to push past her distaste for the sight of bloody injuries. Perhaps she'd be able to keep her focus on the lantern and not look at the wound at all. "Billy Joe," she continued, "you gather those eggs like I told you to, then head inside."

"Are you going to be able to help me without getting faint, Miss Daisy?" Dr. Walker asked. "We don't want to risk you dropping the lantern and setting your barn on fire, do we?" His tone was no-nonsense, but his eyes were kind.

She set her chin. "I'll do what needs to be done, as I always have," she insisted, though her legs already felt like jelly. "Will you have enough light out here with the lantern, or should we move him into the kitchen?"

"Oughta be enough light with that hole up there." The doc nodded toward the gap in the roof that let in the last of the day's light at the moment as the sun slowly set, but allowed rain in as well, whenever the rain came. She was just thankful that hill country in Texas rarely got truly cold, or the draught the hole let in might be harmful to the animals. She knew she should get it fixed. She should do a lot of things to maintain her run-down property.

Daisy acknowledged the barn roof's state of disrepair with a rueful grimace. "I've been meaning to get that roof repaired forever," she muttered. "There just hasn't been any spare cash—or anyone to do it."

Thorn had been quiet, watching both of them as the doctor spoke to her, but now he spoke up. "Maybe I can fix that for you, Mrs. Henderson, before I ride on."

By an effort of will, Daisy kept a skeptical look from her face. Even if he was sincere in his offer—which she doubted, for why would a stranger concern himself with the state of her barn roof?—he must realize there was no feasible way for him to complete the task. It would be a while before he was fit enough to climb up onto her barn roof and repair it. And even then, he'd need to stay hidden, not be working up there in full view of anyone passing by.

"Mmm," muttered the doctor. "I'd best get on with

it, I suppose. Miss Daisy, would you be able to fetch me some clean water, please?"

"Of course. I set some to boil when I sent my son to fetch you, then took it off the fire so it could cool down when I saw that you'd arrived. And there's a spare cot in the tack room—I'll bring out some bedding for it."

"Excellent," Dr. Walker stated. "I didn't like the idea of him lying in the dirty straw with these wounds."

Daisy was grateful for an excuse to get some fresh air before she helped the doctor, even though she had a feeling Nolan Walker would use the time to ask some pointed questions of the stranger in her barn.

She wondered if Thorn would give more answers to the doctor than he'd shared with her. Men tended to do that—hide more troubling details from her, as if she wasn't strong enough to handle the truth. As if she hadn't dealt with an abusive husband, and then the shame of a jailed husband while raising her son on her own. She was stronger than most folks realized. Strong enough to deal with this new complication in her life.

Much later, when the ordeal of cleaning out the wounds with carbolic acid and bandaging them was over, the doctor gave Thorn a dose of laudanum, instructed Daisy about his care and then departed, promising to check on him tomorrow.

Back in the house, she scrambled the eggs and set

a plateful in front of Billy Joe. Then she loaded up a second plate with eggs, a thick slice of fresh bread and some of her preserves.

"Is that for Mr. Thorn?" Billy Joe asked eagerly. "I can take it to him, Ma!"

"Call him Mr. Dawson, honey. And no, I need you to stay put and eat your supper," Daisy ordered.

Billy Joe pouted. "But I thought you wanted me to help take care of him. Wasn't that what you said?"

"I do. And you will. Don't forget what we agreed," she reminded him. "You're to look after Mr. Dawson while I'm at work."

Her shift as cook at the hotel restaurant lasted from dawn until suppertime. She got only half an hour for a break after the midday crowd thinned out. She usually sat down on the back porch and ate whatever could be spared from the leftovers on the stove, while Tilly Pridemore, the waitress, kept an eye on the dining room.

"I'll rush back here during my break," Daisy told her son, "and check on Mr. Dawson then. But you're responsible for seeing to it that he has whatever he needs the rest of the time."

"I *know*, Ma." Billy Joe rolled his eyes. "You already tole me a hunnerd times."

"I don't like that tone, young man. Remember our deal? You promised to be on your best behavior. Have you changed your mind?" *Please, no*, she prayed. *I need this chance to get through to him.*

Billy Joe was a good boy at heart—she knew that as surely as she knew her own name. But even good boys could be persuaded to make bad decisions, especially when their friends were leading the way. If Billy Joe was busy looking after their houseguest, it would keep him away from his troublemaking friends, which had to be a good thing. It might even help her boy learn some responsibility.

"No, ma'am," Billy Joe said meekly. "I'll look after Mr. Dawson real good, I promise."

"And you won't go wandering off with your friends and leave him alone?"

"No way! Not when I can stay here and talk to Mr. Dawson about outlawing." He looked far too excited at the idea, and Daisy winced. Was it foolish of her to leave her son alone with a man who would fill his head with tall tales that would glamorize the wild life of an outlaw? No, she couldn't bring herself to believe that Thorn would do that, not after he had already acknowledged that it wasn't good for the boy to admire outlaws as he did.

"Just see that you don't bother Mr. Dawson when he's trying to rest," she said. "He's going to need time to heal."

"Maybe he'll heal real slow," Billy Joe said hopefully. "Then he can stay for a long time. I want him to stay and teach me stuff!"

"Teach you stuff?" Daisy echoed, aghast. "Such as *what*?"

"Like how to do a fast draw," Billy Joe told her, in a tone that indicated the answer should have been obvious to her.

"What makes you think he's a fast draw?" Daisy asked. Had Thorn Dawson been boasting of gunslinging skills to her impressionable son? Wounds or no wounds, he'd be out of her barn tonight if that was true!

Billy Joe shrugged. "Ma, an outlaw *has* to be a fast draw," he explained with exaggerated patience. "I'll just bet he's good at it, that's all. Fast as lightning. You can tell."

They'd do better to hope the man would heal as fast as lightning—and go on his way before anyone else found out he was here. Mr. Prendergast, the hotel proprietor, wouldn't tolerate even the slightest hint of a scandal when it came to the people he employed. If he found out she was harboring a fugitive, she'd lose her job, and then how would she support herself and her son?

"Ma?" Billy Joe said, interrupting her thoughts. "You sure you don't want me to take that plate out to Mr. Dawson? I'm all done with my supper, see?" He gestured to his plate, which he'd emptied while she'd been woolgathering. The boy always shoveled down food as if he thought it was going to try to run away from him. And he was always hungry for more. Keeping him fed only got more challenging the bigger he grew—and the challenge wouldn't get any easier now that they had another mouth to feed. She'd just have to take it one day at a time.

"No, I'll do it," she insisted. She could tell that the process of cleaning and bandaging his wounds had been painful and exhausting for Thorn. The last thing he needed was an excitable boy bouncing around him, trying to pump him for exciting stories. Picking up the plate, she headed for the door. It was dark now, and she carried a lantern to light her way into the dark barn.

She found Thorn Dawson asleep in the stall on the cot, covered with the spare blanket she'd brought out. He didn't stir when she set the dish of food on a bale of hay and softly called his name. The laudanum must have taken effect faster than she'd expected, on top of the exhaustion the man must already have been experiencing.

He was sleeping on his side, his ribs rising and falling with his soft, regular breathing. Seeing his features relaxed in slumber, Daisy found it impossible to believe this man could be an outlaw. *But appearances could be deceiving, couldn't they?*

It would be best if Thorn left as soon as he was physically able, as he'd said. But she shouldn't be thinking of him by his first name, Thorn, as if he were a friend. He should be strictly "Mr. Dawson" to her, even in her thoughts, Daisy told herself. She didn't know him, not really. And she saw no sense in trying to get to know him when he would just be on his way as soon as he recovered. She'd treat him with courtesy and with simple Christian compassion—no more than that. But no *less* than that, either. Not when she'd decided that it was her Christian duty to care for him.

He'd said he hadn't done the shooting and wasn't really an outlaw, after all. Why, if either of the wounded bank employees took a turn for the worse and died, she could be sending Thorn Dawson to the gallows, even though he wasn't the man who had shot them, Daisy realized. A judge might be so bent on making an example of Mr. Dawson that, innocent or not, he'd pay the ultimate price for another man's actions. She shuddered at the thought of Thorn Dawson with a rope around his neck.

No, she had to help him, even though it would be hard. It was the right thing to do. *Blessed are the merciful*, Jesus had said. So she *was* doing the right thing, wasn't she? She could urge him to turn himself in once he was healed and ready to leave, couldn't she? Sighing at the complexity of the question, Daisy left the barn and returned to the house.

He'd thought at first she was a dream, a vision conjured up by the effects of the laudanum, which fogged his brain and made opening his eyes wider than slits seem impossible. But he'd been aware of her presence and had even stolen a peek when she turned to stare at his wounded leg and shoulder, both now all properly cleaned up and bandaged.

Daisy. He'd heard the doctor call her that. *The name suited her.* Thorn could see that she'd been a beautiful woman once—and could be again, if someone cared enough to look after her. That careworn look would fade, he knew, with the right man at her side. Evidently, Billy Joe's father hadn't been the right man, not by a long shot, but Thorn could tell Daisy Henderson was a good mother to her son.

Suddenly—and quite illogically—he wondered what it would be like to be that right man for her, and for her boy. But there was no way that could happen. Not with him living a lie, pretending to be one of the Griggs gang. And not even as his true self, an officer of the law, constantly gone on missions to keep the peace.

He'd been so proud, so happy when he'd become a Texas Ranger. He'd been confident that his work would help make Texas a better, safer place. But he wasn't a Texas Ranger anymore, he reminded himself. Not officially. There were no Texas Rangers— they had been disbanded when the carpetbaggers' government took over the reins after Texas's defeat in the War Between the States, and E. J. Davis, the new governor, had set up a new police department. The State Police were largely despised as tools of the Reconstruction government. Moreover, most of the men were motivated by greed rather than by an honest desire to serve, which meant that far too many were open to bribes and other dirty dealings. Instead of acting as an effective force against the growing lawlessness in the state, they were, in fact, part of the problem. But a Ranger leader whom Thorn respected, Leander McNelly, had encouraged him to join the State Police, anyway.

"Better times are coming, Dawson," McNelly had told him. "This carpetbag Federal government won't keep Texas under its thumb forever, and when it loses its grip, we'll want to be able to start the Rangers up again. So go ahead and join the State Police if they'll have you, and you can be our eyes and ears till those better times come. This way there'll be at least one officer that's not corrupt."

The State Police had accepted his application, either because they were too disorganized to investigate his background and realize he'd been a Texas Ranger, or because there were others doing the same thing. It was a living, Thorn supposed, but it was quite a comedown from the real thing. Instead of keeping bandits out of the state, they were used as instruments to keep the conquered Texans afraid and compliant. It had been a relief when his division had been tasked with bringing down the notorious Griggs gang, and Thorn had agreed to go and join the gang to report on their movements.

So now I am a Ranger in disguise, disguised fur-

ther as an outlaw, he mused. It was enough to make his head ache, trying to remember who he really was.

What he did know was that Daisy Henderson was a lady, as well as a kind and generous woman, and he was in no position to court her. But perhaps he could do some good while he stayed here, even if that "good" consisted only of providing temporary mentoring to a boy sorely in need of a father's guiding hand.

Thunder rolled overhead, and a moment later rain began to patter on the roof overhead—*or what's left of it*, he thought, as several drops found their way onto his head from above. Yes sir, if he stayed here, he was going to have to find a way to fix that roof for Daisy Henderson.

Groaning with the effort, he raised himself off the cot and dragged it to the side a few inches so the rain fell next to him, rather than on him. In doing so, he found the cloth-covered plate of food she'd left on the bale of hay, complete with a fork to eat with.

"Well, that's a mighty fine reason to get out of bed," he murmured, as the scent of the eggs and the sight of fresh bread and a little heap of preserves met his nose and eyes and set his mouth to watering.

As he pulled the plate onto his lap and put a forkful of eggs into his mouth, Thorn blessed Daisy Henderson for her kindness. And he vowed that he would never do anything to make her regret it.

* * *

Inside, Daisy was still trying to satisfy the curiosity of her wakeful son and prevent him from going out to the barn to check on their "guest."

"So did the doctor have to dig a bullet outta Mr. Dawson, Ma?" Billy Joe inquired. "Do ya think he might give it to me, if he did?"

"Dr. Walker gave the bullet from his shoulder to Mr. Dawson," Daisy told her son patiently, while hiding her dismay at his eagerness for gory details. She knew the boy would think Mr. Dawson had a greater right to the bullet than he did. "The leg wound was just a graze, as he'd thought."

Billy Joe's face fell. "But do ya think he'll let me look at the bullet? I'd give it back, honest! And maybe he'd let me see his gun? Or I could—"

Daisy had had enough of this conversation. "The only thing you're going to do tonight is head straight to bed. We've had enough excitement for one day and my shift at the restaurant starts at 6:00 a.m., you know, even if you get to sleep later. Settle down now and close your eyes."

"Okay, Ma," he muttered.

She leaned over and gave him a kiss on the top of his tousled head, and was rewarded with a grin. She was glad that at twelve, Billy Joe wasn't yet too old for such motherly attention, and she hoped he never would grow too old to enjoy a mother's kiss. He also wasn't too old to try to break the rules, if he thought he could get away with it. She wouldn't put it past her son to sneak out to "check" on Thorn, so she'd have to sleep with her ears open for the telltale creak of the floorboards.

She started for the door, then had a thought. "Billy Joe, if you want Mr. Dawson to remain safe, you can't be telling all your friends that he's in the barn— not even one of them, you hear?" It was clear to her from her son's startled expression that he had been thinking about doing just that—putting Thorn Dawson on display in their barn for an audience of his admiring pals. "You tell *anyone*, and the next thing you know it'll be all over town and the sheriff will put Mr. Dawson in jail." And her reputation would be in tatters while her job would be long gone. But she couldn't expect her son to fully understand that, or why it would matter.

"Of course I won't tell anyone, Ma. Mum's the word," he said, shutting his mouth and turning an imaginary key in an imaginary lock there.

"Good boy. I love you, Billy Joe. Good night."

"Love you, too, Ma. Good night." He shut his eyes, and a moment later his regular breathing told Daisy that her son had surrendered to slumber.

But it was a long time before she slept. She couldn't quite get Thorn Dawson's face out of her mind, nor the change his arrival had made in her humdrum existence. It would not be a change that lasted very long, she knew. As soon as he recovered, he would ride out of Simpson Creek and out of their lives, and her dreary life would go on as before. It was the same return to humdrumness her son was dreading, she realized with a pang.

At times she wished her life could be less dreary, she admitted, but all the changes she had ever pondered making in her existence meant the chance of danger. And she'd never considered exposing herself and her son to danger worth the risk. They faced far too much danger already. If she could just keep herself and her son safe and secure, then she wouldn't dare dream of asking for anything more.

Chapter Three

After waking briefly when dawn light began to steal through the hole in the roof, Thorn had dozed again, only to be awakened by the arrival of breakfast. Based by the light angling through the battered roof, it seemed to be a few hours later. His plate of food was not delivered by Daisy Henderson as he'd hoped, but by her eager-eyed, energetic son, who brought his own breakfast with him. "So ya won't have t' eat alone, Mr. Dawson," he explained.

"Where's your mother?"

"Ma's been at the hotel restaurant workin' for least an hour now," Billy Joe responded. "She has to get up afore the roosters t' fix breakfast for the hotel guests and anyone else who happens to come into the restaurant. She left us menfolk our breakfasts on the stove and a note that I was to bring yours to ya soon as I got up."

Thorn suppressed a smile at the boy's labeling himself as a man. Without a father or older brother to look up to, Billy Joe probably did think of himself as the man of the house.

It was hard to be disappointed that Daisy hadn't brought it, given the presence of this cheerful boy, who obviously thought eating with Thorn was a high privilege. But had she chosen Billy Joe to perform the task because she was in a hurry, or because she was avoiding Thorn?

"Your ma's a good cook," he murmured, savoring the taste of the crisp bacon and the perfectly scrambled eggs, despite the fact he'd had the same for supper. "The hotel's mighty lucky to have her working for them."

"She's been the cook since mean ol' Mrs. Powell died," Billy Joe informed him. "Before that she was a waitress there, and we didn't ever think she'd get to be the cook, 'cause it seemed like Mrs. Powell would probably keep the job until she was a hunnerd," Billy Joe reported. "But she died, and that was good, 'cause a cook makes more money and we needed some more of that around here."

"You sound pretty glad that the woman died," Thorn commented drily.

Billy Joe had the grace to look ashamed. "I'm glad Ma got the job, but I'd have been just as glad 'bout that if Mrs. Powell had quit or moved away or somethin'. I'm not glad she died." He paused, then added stubbornly, "But I ain't all that sad, either. She was old and mean, and she treated my ma bad. I don't like anyone bein' mean to Ma."

"I reckon I can understand that," Thorn said. "So now she's treated better at the restaurant?"

Billy Joe shrugged. "Some better. She gets paid more, so that's good. But there's still that nasty old Mr. Prendergast, the proprietor," he explained. "He's real bossy. Always fussing over every little thing, like he's lookin' for a reason to complain or to tell Ma that whatever she's doin', she's doin' it wrong. Never happy with nothin'. And Ma thinks the lady who's the waitress now, Miss Tilly, wants her job— to be the cook, I mean. Miss Tilly's always braggin' about the great dishes she can make. But I've had her cookin' some now and then and her food ain't got nuthin' on Ma's," the boy declared loyally.

There was always some bad apple at a workplace making trouble for others because they were jealous or spiteful, Thorn thought. And that was not count-ing the problems that came from an overly particu-lar boss. As much as he disliked his current task, he was glad he had some independence in the way he made his living. It would drive him loco to work in an office somewhere and have some boss always looking over his shoulder.

From what little he had seen so far, Thorn judged Daisy Henderson to be a proud woman, not a com-plainer—especially in front of her son, for whom she seemed to want to set a good example. So if the boy had surmised that much about her workplace problems, Thorn suspected she was ill-treated indeed. Which went further to explain the woman's careworn expression, and once again he wished he were in a position to do something about it.

"Tell me 'bout the outlaw life, Mr. Dawson," Billy Joe pleaded around a mouthful of eggs. "Bet you've had some great times."

Thorn winced inwardly. There it was, the very thing Daisy had voiced a fear of: her son thinking that being an outlaw was glamorous and exciting. Maybe the one thing that he could do for her would be to nip that idea in the bud and turn Billy Joe onto a better path.

"A few," he said. "A very few good times, and a lot more times when being an outlaw was dangerous and dirty and we were hungry and cold—or hot— and tired of running and hiding from honest folks."

The boy's eyes clouded with suspicion. "Ma told you to say that, didn't she? She don't want me to be an outlaw, but wants me to grow up to be a clerk at a stuffy ol' store, or somethin' like that."

"But that's not what you want," Thorn said, dodging the question.

The boy screwed up his face. "Naw, what kinda life is *that*?" he asked, his voice disdainful. "I'd rather be out ridin' free, with no one to tell me what to do. Like you do."

If the boy only knew. "But whoever led the out-laws would tell you what to do," Thorn pointed out.

"Yeah, of course. Somebody has to be the leader," Billy Joe agreed. "But if I was the bravest and fast-est and smartest of the gang, pretty soon *I'd* get to be the leader, right? And all the men would have to do what *I* said."

"Maybe…" Thorn said, picturing Griggs, the head of the gang he'd been riding with for the past two weeks, who was easily the laziest and most cowardly, selfish man he'd ever met. Griggs never risked his own hide if he could order one of his men to do the chancy jobs. Smart, though—he definitely was that. As cunning as a snake, and every bit as mean. His men didn't necessarily look up to him or respect him, but they did fear him, and he used that fear to keep them in line—for now.

"Usually someone has to die before there's a new leader," Thorn murmured. "And until you were in charge, what about having to steal from a nice lady like your ma? You'd have to do it if the leader said so," he added, when he saw doubt creep into the boy's eyes.

"I'd never let no outlaw steal from my ma," the boy insisted. "Not ever."

"But you'd steal from someone else's ma? Any lady you robbed might have a boy of her own, wait-ing for her to bring that money home. What are they to do if you take that money away?" Billy Joe didn't have an answer for that, so Thorn let him chew on it for a bit before attacking the argument from another angle, one he hoped would be even more persuasive.

"I reckon you'd like to get married someday, wouldn't you? Find a nice lady like your ma and have sons of your own? Daughters, too."

"Well, sure. I'd settle down some day, after I'd had enough outlawin'… Amelia Collier at school, one of the twins, said she'd marry me when we grew up if I stayed around Simpson Creek," he said proudly. "She's pretty and sweet, and her father owns a big ranch outside of town."

"You think Mr. Collier would let his daughter have anything to do with a man who used to be an outlaw? A man with a price on his head, who'd robbed folks, maybe killed someone?"

Billy Joe was quiet. "I'd never kill no one, 'less they were bad. And I wouldn't hurt nobody here, anyway. I'd go away somewheres, and have some fun where there ain't nobody I know to stop me, or to tell my ma mean stories of what I done an' make her sad. I'd be far away, till I'd had my fill of outlawin', and then this here town is where I'd come home to. But I ain't ready to be stuck here for the rest of my life just yet. I wanna get out and see the country— maybe the world, even."

Thorn couldn't argue with that hunger to see what the world looked like outside of the place where you were born and raised. He'd been eager to escape from his home and his father's bitterness, though he'd stayed in Texas and protected the state against the Indians during the war years.

Other young men he knew had gone to the army, eager to see a bit of the country. He'd heard many a sad tale of what they had encountered from those who returned—and of course, there were many of them who had never made it home to boast of all that they had witnessed.

During Thorn's own travels, he'd seen many different places, and found that the world outside of his hometown wasn't so very different from what he'd known before. No matter where he went, some people were kind and others were cruel. Some spots were beautiful and others were ugly. Some folks were happy and settled, while others were restless and sad. That was just life, no matter what scenery surrounded it.

The only thing that truly made one place more special than any other was having people there who loved you, and who you loved. That was what made a place a home—and it wasn't something Thorn had had in a long, long time. Billy Joe had that right here, with a mother who would clearly do anything for him, but he was too young to really appreciate it. The grass wasn't always greener on the other side of the fence, but Thorn would never convince this boy of that.

"You could serve in the army for a spell," he

pointed out. "You'd see some sights that way, then you could come home and marry your Amelia, knowing you had your good name and something to be proud of."

"Join the army? Then I'd have to take orders all the time," Billy Joe said, his voice scornful. "Besides, I'm a Texas boy—no way I'd join up with a bunch of bluebellies tellin' me what to do."

Thorn couldn't suppress a wry smile. "Billy Joe, unless you're the president or a king or something, you're always going to be told what to do by someone," he said. Come to think of it, he doubted even presidents or kings really got to do whatever they wanted; they had too many responsibilities on their plate for that. "That's part of living, and being a man." But he could tell the boy wasn't convinced.

While he was still wondering how to persuade Billy Joe that being an outlaw wasn't all it was cracked up to be, he heard footsteps outside. Tensing, he reached for the Colt he'd left under his pillow—and found it was no longer there. Had Daisy Henderson disarmed him, while he was under the powerful influence of laudanum? He couldn't exactly blame her for taking the precaution, but it left him feeling entirely too exposed. As injured as he was, he couldn't fight his way out of trouble with his fists. He needed his gun. Foolish, to have let his desire to be free of pain put him in such a vulnerable position.

He hadn't long to wait to see who it was. A mo-

ment later Dr. Walker pushed the creaking door aside
and stepped into the stall. But he wasn't alone. A tall,
well-built man with a tin star on his chest followed.

Thorn stiffened. He'd hoped the doctor would
keep his presence here a secret, as he had requested,
but Walker hadn't. Evidently his concern for the
town's safety overrode his promise.

Thorn couldn't argue with the man's priorities. In
Walker's place, he'd have done the same.

Billy Joe's face went white with shock, his eyes
gleaming with anger at the betrayal. He'd have to be
careful here, Thorn thought. Billy Joe was already
inclined to sympathize more with lawbreakers than
with the men who upheld justice and order. And if
he saw Thorn, whom he seemed to like and respect,
hauled away by the sheriff, it would just worsen his
opinion of lawmen.

"Mornin', Dawson. I see you made it through the
night all right," the doctor said in his breezy Yan-
kee accent. It had been quite a surprise to hear it
the previous evening. To distract Thorn from the
pain of having his wounds cleaned and bandaged,
the doctor had told him the story of how he'd grown
up in Maine, but then befriended a Confederate col-
onel who had been badly wounded near the end of
the war. The doc had explained how he'd helped his
friend journey home to Texas once the war was finally over, and had found himself falling in love with
the state and choosing to make it his home. That he'd

found love with a Texas belle in Simpson Creek had merely cemented it. "How's the pain?"

"Tolerable," Thorn said, his eyes darting from the Billy Joe to the Simpson Creek sheriff. "Billy Joe, go back in the house." He didn't want the boy to be present when the lawman led him off with the come-alongs he saw sticking out of his back pocket.

Billy Joe had evidently seen them, too. He leaped to his feet and faced the sheriff, fists clenched at his sides. "No! You can't take Mr. Dawson! He ain't one of the ones you're really after, one of them men who went firing off their guns—he didn't shoot nobody!" Billy Joe cried. "Besides, he's wounded! He needs to be here where we kin take care of 'im!"

"Billy Joe, I said go into the house," Thorn said, keeping his voice calm, even as he kept an eye on the sheriff. "Remember, we were just talking about how a man always has to take orders from someone, and this is one of those times," he said. "Go inside, and everything will be all right."

Billy Joe whirled to face Thorn. "I won't let him take you!" he cried, red-faced now with fury. "I *won't*!"

"Billy Joe, I said to *go inside*," Thorn repeated. "Please." His eyes dueled with the boy's for a long moment, then all at once Billy Joe abruptly turned away and ran out of the barn. A moment later the sound of a door slamming door reached their ears.

Thorn guessed the boy had been close to tears, and hadn't wanted anyone to see that.

He glanced at the sheriff, then turned to the doctor.

"Dawson, this is Sheriff Bishop," Dr. Walker said. "I thought it best to apprise him of your presence, and let him hear your side of the story."

"I understand, Doctor. Sheriff." Thorn acknowledged the lawman with a nod.

Dr. Walker said, "While I'm cleaning and changing these bandages on your wounds, why don't you ask him your questions, Sheriff?" He set his bag down in the straw.

"Yeah, I could use the distraction," Thorn said. "The doc's carbolic stings a mite." He said it with a grin, wanting to lighten the grim, cold look in the sheriff's eyes, but the ice in them didn't melt one little bit. *Good for him.* Clearly, the man was nobody's fool. And he took his job and his responsibility to the town seriously, exactly as he should. But that admirable toughness might make it difficult for Thorn to turn the sheriff into an ally.

"All I know so far is what the doctor told me you said yesterday—that you've been riding with the Griggs gang, taking part in their robberies and raids, but you claim not to be one of them," Bishop challenged. "Is that true?"

"Yes, sir, it is."

"Then suppose you tell me right now what you

were doing, robbing a bank with them yesterday? If you're going to stay here in my town while you recover, then I need more of an explanation than I've gotten so far. Unless you want to receive the rest of your care in one of my jail cells, that is," he added.

Thorn raised a hand—the one that wasn't clenched into a fist, since the doctor was sponging that burning liquid over the wound in his shoulder—to indicate he was willing to talk, as soon as he could do so without groaning.

"I'm working for the State Police," he said eventually. "My orders are to infiltrate the Griggs gang so that I can warn the authorities where the gang is likely to strike next. The goal is to set a trap to catch them in the act, so they can be brought to justice." He kept his eyes locked on Bishop's, and as he expected, suspicion remained in the lawman's steady gaze. "You don't have to believe me," Thorn said. "You can telegraph the State Police headquarters in Austin. Address it to Captain Hepplewhite and he'll confirm my identity and my assignment."

"You're working with the State Police," Bishop repeated, with the same curl to his lip he might have had if Thorn had said he was employed by Ulysses S. Grant or William Sherman.

"Yes, although at heart I still consider myself to be a Texas Ranger rather than a state policeman. I was a Ranger and stayed here to protect Texas rather than going off to war, and God willing, I'll be able to call myself a Ranger again someday."

He thought the frost melted a little in Bishop's eyes at his last remark, but the lawman's tone was as cold as ever when he spoke again. "If that was the plan, why weren't you able to warn us before our bank was robbed?"

"I just joined the gang a fortnight ago. Griggs doesn't fully trust me yet, so he doesn't confide his plans to me," Thorn said. "His closest men watch me like a hawk. Reckon it'll take a while before they trust me enough so that I'll know of a holdup far enough ahead of time that I can sneak away to warn the law. Meanwhile, my orders are to play along with whatever the gang chooses to do, so that I can win their trust, while avoiding harming the citizenry, of course."

"Sounds like the kind of harebrained scheme the carpetbag government police would come up with," Bishop said with a sneer. "What makes you think they'll ever trust you that much, if you're not shooting innocent people right along with them? Maybe they're just playing along, pretending to trust you, till they catch you ratting on them."

His last remark played right into Thorn's deepest fear. He'd been warned that the plan was dangerous, that the Griggs gang would show no mercy if they found him out.

"Maybe they are," he agreed. "It's the chance I've

agreed to take." The gang would just continue hurting decent people until they were stopped. Thorn might not be proud to say he was a state policeman, but he'd certainly be proud to play a role in stopping Griggs and his gang. And besides, it wasn't as if anyone would miss him if he failed and paid the ultimate price.

He'd thought his last admission would be enough to satisfy Bishop, but evidently the lawman was even harder than he appeared, for his gaze remained narrowed. "What makes a fellow willing to take such a risk as you're taking, Dawson? Money?" he murmured, in a tone that suggested the topic was of only mild interest—though the intensity in his eyes told a different story.

"They'll pay me well enough, if I succeed," Thorn drawled, in that same careless tone the sheriff had used.

"Maybe so, but I don't believe that's all there is to it," Bishop shot back. "What is it you're atoning for?"

The man was too shrewd. Thorn shifted his gaze, hoping the other man hadn't seen the wince that gave away how accurate the shot-in-the-dark question had been, and set his jaw. "I reckon that's my business, Sheriff, especially since it has nothing to do with the Simpson Creek bank or anything else about this town. And I'll tell you right now that Mrs. Henderson and her boy have nothing to fear from me."

He kept his eye staring unblinkingly at the man,

hoping the sheriff could see how deeply and truly he meant the words. After a long moment, the lawman shrugged. "You can keep your secrets, Dawson. But you go back on your word and do one ounce of harm to Mrs. Henderson and her boy, or anyone else in this town, and I'll make you wish you'd never been born."

Thorn could tell the sheriff meant what he said. Good thing he'd rather die than harm one hair on Daisy Henderson's head—or Billy Joe's. But couldn't his presence here potentially harm her by sullying her reputation? He'd have to remedy that as soon as he was able—by leaving once he'd recovered enough to be able to ride again.

"By the way, Dr. Walker, how're your other patients doing? The teller and the bank president, I mean?" Thorn asked. In truth, he had been worried about the two bank robbery victims, but he also hoped his query would further strengthen the evidence that he was a good man.

Dr. Walker looked pleased that Thorn had inquired, but Sheriff Bishop showed not so much as a flicker of approval. The man would be an excellent cardsharp, if he ever decided to give up being a lawman, Thorn thought. His face revealed nothing.

Fine with Thorn. He wasn't here to make friends. He was here to see Griggs and all his miserable thugs land in jail where they belonged. And the sooner he could get back to that task, the better.

* * *

"When did you become such a clock watcher, Daisy?" Tilly inquired, as Daisy dished up yet another helping of the day's special, chicken and dumplings, and handed it to the waitress.

Daisy wrenched her gaze away from the clock on the shelf above the sink. "I don't mean to be," she said. Trust the other woman to notice if Daisy's attention wandered off of her work for so much as a second. Tilly seemed to resent even the brief half hour Daisy could call her own during the workday, even though she received her own work break right after Daisy returned, during which time Daisy had to take on the waitressing as well as the cooking. "I just need to go home on my break to check on things, that's all."

"Things" meant the wounded man in her barn, of course. Had she been right to leave him to her son's care? Though he'd been asleep, she had thought that Dawson had looked well enough when she'd left for work. She hadn't seen any indication that an infection was troubling him, or that he was sleeping poorly. But who knew what could happen in her absence? Maybe his wound had reopened, causing him to bleed to death, or maybe a fever had spiked and he'd died. But no, surely Billy Joe would have run to report to her if any calamity had happened. She'd told him to let her know if there was a problem. Had the doctor returned to check on his patient this morning as he'd promised to?

She knew why she was worrying so much. It wasn't really because of the man himself, but because of the memories he stirred of Peter. She still blamed herself—would always blame herself—for the way her brother's injury had led to his death when she was supposed to be looking after him. She couldn't let that happen to Thorn—that is, to Mr. Dawson.

"That boy of yours causing you worry again? Better nip his mischief in the bud, or he'll turn out just as bad as his daddy," Tilly opined with a triumphant gleam in her eye. She seemed never happier than when she managed to find a new opportunity to remind Daisy of all the shortcomings of her late husband. As if she could ever forget. The scars—both the physical marks and the bruises he'd left on her heart and her soul—would never go away.

Sometimes Daisy missed Mrs. Powell, who had been the cook when she herself was a waitress. The older woman had been a crank and a bully, but her bullying tactics hadn't been so full of innuendo and malice as Tilly's were. Besides, Mrs. Powell had seemed to hate just about everyone, so spread her vitriol around generously, insulting and belittling everyone who crossed her path. Tilly had only one target, and struck it as often as she could.

Daisy wished no one had ever told Tilly about her

late husband when the waitress had moved to town after her own engagement to a local rancher had been broken off. But in such a small community it was inevitable someone would have told the younger woman Daisy's sad marital history. After all, everyone knew he had been an abusive tyrant—toward her and Billy Joe, and toward the schoolteacher who William had eventually gone to jail for attacking. For most people in town, that history was a reason to treat her with kindness and compassion, showing understanding for the difficulties she'd faced. But with Tilly, any flaw or shortcoming in Daisy was something to be pounced on and mocked.

"Billy Joe's been good as gold," Daisy replied, striving to keep the defensive note out of her voice, even after Tilly's face took on a skeptical look at her assertion. "It's just that I had set him to a task, and I want to make sure he did what I told him to." That wasn't a lie, was it? She *had* given him the task of watching over the wounded man, after all.

Tilly bent to peer out the narrow opening of the serving window between the kitchen and the dining room. "Looks like all the noon crowd's gone, so go ahead and take your break, why don't you? Reckon I can handle anyone who happens to mosey in while you're away. But you won't be late getting back to prepare supper, will you? Mr. Prendergast might come in to check, and you know he'd ask when you left. I wouldn't want to lie." She made no attempt to hide the malice in her tone, and Daisy knew Tilly would be delighted to have any opportunity to show her in a poor light to their employer.

Daisy stifled a huff of exasperation, not wanting the other woman to see that the needling had gotten under Daisy's skin. Of course Tilly would think tattling to their boss would further her ambition to replace Daisy as cook.

"You've never had to cover for my lateness, and today will be no different," Daisy said evenly. She pulled off her hotel apron. It was all she could do to keep from running out the door, but she managed to walk casually until she was out of sight of the hotel.

She concentrated on looking calm and at ease, but in truth she was a bundle of nerves, worrying about the state she'd find Dawson in when she returned home. And those nerves only got worse when she got further down the road and caught sight of two men heading in the opposite direction: Dr. Walker and Sheriff Bishop.

Were they coming from her place? Had the sheriff discovered she was sheltering a fugitive?

Chapter Four

"I saw Doc Walker and Sheriff Bishop walking back toward town from this direction," Daisy said by way of greeting as her eyes adjusted to the dusty gloom of the barn.

"They were just here," Thorn said, answering her unspoken question.

"And…?" She couldn't believe the sheriff hadn't insisted Thorn do the rest of his recovering in a jail cell.

Her patient shrugged. "The sawbones said I was healing up well as could be expected, though he thought the wounds looked a little inflamed. And the lawman told me to watch my step around you," Thorn added evenly, his expression giving away nothing. "The sheriff knows why I was riding with the outlaws, ma'am, and I believe I satisfied him that he has no cause to worry about your safety or Billy

Joe's, as far as I'm concerned. He says the bank president and teller are recovering well, too."

Relieved, Daisy let out a sigh, feeling tension draining from her shoulders. But along with the relief was curiosity, wondering what he had told Bishop that he hadn't told her. The town sheriff wasn't an easy man to satisfy when it came to anyone or anything that threatened the safety of Simpson Creek, Yet Dawson had apparently managed to set his concerns to rest, at least for the time being. It was an impressive feat, and it made her feel a little better about her own decision to let Dawson stay. Even if he didn't feel he could share his full story with her, the fact that the sheriff was content with it gave her a real sense of comfort.

Suddenly the sound of his stomach rumbling in the silence reminded her that it was long past noon and the man before her might be hungry. "Here," she said, reaching inside her reticule and bringing out the plate of chicken and dumplings she'd wrapped in heavy paper and brought from the hotel, careful to carry it so that the food wouldn't spill over the plate inside its wrapping. She'd stopped at the house long enough to fetch a fork and napkin from her own kitchen, knowing she didn't dare borrow them from the hotel under Tilly's all-seeing gaze. As it was, she'd have to make sure the waitress saw her bring the plate back. It would be all too like the woman to spread a rumor that she'd stolen it. "I brought your dinner."

He eyed it, but made no move to take it from her. "Did you already eat at the hotel?"

She dropped her gaze from his. "No. But I'm not hungry," she added too quickly before her stomach betrayed her by rumbling, too.

"Miss Daisy, it's not nice to fib to your guest, even out of politeness," he chided gently. "That's your dinner, isn't it?"

She nodded, eyes still downcast. She hadn't dared take more than the usual modest portion she usually consumed, for if she'd placed a hearty man-size portion on the plate, Tilly might have noticed and suspected that something was up. And if her suspicions were raised, she was the sort to poke and prod until she found an answer. Once Tilly started digging around to try to find answers, Daisy might as well invite the waitress home to meet Thorn Dawson there and then, because there would be no hiding the secret from her any longer. Nor would there be any way to keep her from spreading the story all over town, and putting the worst, most damaging slant on it that she could. The only way to prevent that disaster was to keep Tilly from suspecting anything at all, for as long as Daisy could.

"Then why don't you sit down here and eat it?" he said, gesturing toward the cot.

"Oh no... I couldn't..." she mumbled.

"Couldn't what, eat in front of me? Just because you don't have enough for both of us? Please, don't let that stop you. It hasn't been all that long since I ate that big breakfast you left for me, so I'm not hungry, but sounds like you are. You'd be keeping me company," he coaxed.

Uneasily, she sat down on the end of the cot. "What…what's Billy Joe doing?" she said. "I expected to find him in here with you. I hope he hasn't been plaguing you with his chatter."

"Not a bit," Thorn assured her. "He brought me my breakfast just as you instructed, then went back in the house when the sheriff and the doc came. You might find he's gone back for more shut-eye. Growing boys like him need their sleep."

Her patient was probably right, Daisy realized. Billy Joe seemed able to stay awake all night if one of his pals loaned him a penny dreadful to read, but he could be almost impossible to wake up in the morning. Some days when she had to go to work before it was time to get him out of bed, she'd awakened him, only to learn later that he'd fallen back to sleep after she'd left, and was tardy to class. At least school was out for the summer and she didn't have to worry about that problem right now.

Thorn gestured toward her little paper-wrapped plate. "Come on, open that up and eat your meal. As a mother of a boy like Billy Joe, you've got to keep up your strength."

The truth of that made her smile, and she obediently unwrapped the chicken and dumplings. "All right, then." She hoped he wouldn't just silently watch her eat—she couldn't imagine swallowing a bite under his dark-eyed regard.

"Why don't you tell me some more about yourself?" she asked him, to turn the focus away from herself.

He smiled as if he sensed her need for diversion, and was willing to indulge her. "What would you like to know?"

"Well..." she said, searching for something to ask. "Start at the beginning. Where are you from?"

His smile tightened a bit, as if this was a painful subject, but he answered readily enough. "My sisters and I were raised on a hardscrabble ranch near Mason, Texas."

"Sisters?"

At that, he relaxed a bit. "Yes, ma'am—a whole passel of them. I have five sisters."

"No brothers?

"No, I'm the only boy."

"Are your sisters older or younger than you?"

"All older. My parents kept trying for a boy, you see, and finally they got me. But my ma, she passed on when I was young. My sisters were the ones to raise me, really." He kept her entertained for the next bit with stories about his antics as a child, and the struggles his sisters had getting him to behave. "As soon as I was old enough, my pa was putting me to work. I learned responsibility and hard work early, but that just meant that any little bit of time that I had free, I was looking to find some mischief to get myself into. I'm sure I was quite a trial to my sisters, but they were always very good to me, all the same."

"Is your family still there out by Mason?"

"They sure are, though they're not still on the ranch itself. All my sisters married, and that meant they had to go where their husbands could find work, or where they could acquire some land. I'm just thankful that none of them had to go too far. There wasn't enough of our ranch to split it between all of us, so my father left the whole property to me. He passed on some years ago, so one of my sisters, Ellanora and her husband, Hap, are living on the ranch now. They're holding it until the day I return to live there."

"And that's what you plan to do when you're—" Daisy tried to find a delicate way to bring up the outlawing that was occupying him and keeping him from his ranch for now "—through with the gang?" she concluded.

"That's been the plan," he agreed. "Ellanora always said the house was mine whenever I wanted it, but I'll probably just build another house either for them and their young'uns or a smaller house just for me. Either way, I reckon I'll add their names to the property deed, since it wouldn't be right to make them start over somewhere new when they've taken good care of my ranch so long."

How very decent of him, she thought, but then everything this man did seemed to be decent and fair. She just didn't understand how he came to be an outlaw—and at the same time, *not* an outlaw, if his word could be believed. She hoped she would get the full story someday.

Daisy thought she noted a certain wistfulness in his face when he spoke of his ranch. "Do you think you'll go back to live there soon?" she asked.

His gaze left hers and he stared into a shadowy corner of the stall and shrugged. "Maybe. Ranching's hard work, so I don't want to wait until I'm too old to do it. And what I'm doing now…well, a fellow doesn't want to stay in it too long. It's the kind of work that can be dangerous if he's pushed himself too far or overstayed his welcome…"

Was he doing that now, overstaying his welcome? Daisy wondered. She wouldn't force him to leave, not before he was recovered, but that didn't change the fact that he was making her life more dangerous every day that he stayed. Why was he lying here, wounded, in her barn? If it was true that he wasn't an outlaw, what sort of dangerous game was he involved in, and why couldn't he simply tell her the truth? Didn't she deserve that?

Suddenly, she had to know. "Thorn, then why—"

"Now you know all about me," he said quickly,

before she could complete her question, "so I think it's time you told me at least a little about yourself."

Oh, I hardly think I know all about you. But she guessed he wasn't ready to tell her any more now, at least. Perhaps he never would be.

"There's very little to tell," she said, also shrugging. "My parents settled in Simpson Creek shortly after it was founded, and I grew up here. I met my husband when he attended a social put on at the church—he'd just come to Simpson Creek to live— and we were married shortly afterward. Why, I didn't even know his middle name till we were standing up in front of the reverend," she added with a little laugh that contained no mirth. *Marry in haste, repent at leisure.*

"Which was…?"

At first she didn't understand what Thorn was asking, and her confusion must have shown, for he added, "His middle name?"

"Oh! Wilbur," she said, with a brief smile. *William Wilbur Henderson.* She'd almost laughed out loud, right there at the altar, when the reverend had first said it. It was fortunate for her that she hadn't, though it wasn't until some days later that she'd learned how dangerous laughing at her new husband could be. How dangerous doing anything around William could be, if he was in the wrong sort of mood.

"What did he do? To make his living, I mean," Thorn asked.

Daisy was glad he'd clarified his question. For a second she'd panicked, thinking Billy Joe might have mentioned that his father had died in prison, and Dawson wanted to know the crime he'd committed. Or that maybe he'd already guessed how abusive her husband had been and was asking what he had done to her. She wasn't ready to talk about that yet. Perhaps she never would be.

"Oh, this and that," she said, trying to sound airy, as if the years of uncertainty and privation while she waited for her husband to settle into a career had never happened. "He helped build the mercantile, worked at the saloon for a while... He could do lots of things." But sticking with a job wasn't one of them. He wasn't incapable, but he'd been lazy and unreliable—not to mention driven by a mean temper. Sooner or later he'd get offended by something his boss required of him, or start spending more time drinking than he did working... She'd gotten used to having little money to buy necessities, to selling family heirlooms she'd brought into the marriage just to make ends meet. Fortunately, her husband didn't mind providing for them through things like hunting and fishing, and was fairly good at both tasks. And Daisy had worked hard at keeping a vegetable garden. So they hadn't ever gone hungry, at least.

She'd thought he would change when she'd succeeded at giving him a son, naming him after his father. Wasn't that what every man wanted, a son to carry on his name and his legacy? And for a time William Henderson *was* a better man—made an effort to be a good husband and father—but eventually Billy Joe's existence only gave him another person on whom to take out his frustrations. On his good days, he was a neglectful and uncaring parent, showing no interest in his son's activities. And on his bad days, well... She'd done her best to put herself between William and Billy Joe, to shield her son to the best of her abilities, but when her boy had gotten older, he'd turned protective of her in turn. And there hadn't been much a little boy could do to stop a grown man other than try to draw William's attention to himself.

Through it all, she'd kept silent about her troubles, for she'd been raised to believe a lady didn't air her dirty laundry outside the family. Caroline Wallace, Billy Joe's schoolteacher and Daisy's friend, had suspected the boy was being abused when she'd been hired by the town two years ago, but it wasn't until Daisy's husband had gotten involved in that horrible plot to kidnap Caroline that William Henderson's true character had come to light for everyone in Simpson Creek.

To her relief, the townspeople had known Daisy wasn't responsible for or in any way complicit with her husband's misdeeds. They'd realized that she feared her husband, with good cause, and had given her a sum of money to resettle herself and her son elsewhere if she wanted so her husband couldn't find them when he was released from jail. But since he'd been killed in a prison riot long before his sentence was up, moving away hadn't been necessary. Determined to make her own way, Daisy had used only a small portion of the money she'd been given, leaving the rest hidden away in case of an emergency, so it would last as long as possible.

"I… I'm sorry," Thorn murmured. "I didn't mean to make you sad."

She hadn't even noticed the tears that had escaped her stinging eyes, but now she felt their wetness streaking down her cheeks. Embarrassed that she'd given in to weakness in front of this near stranger, Daisy reached for the handkerchief she kept in one of the deep pockets in her skirt and dabbed at her face.

Darting a glance at Thorn, she saw the awkward expression he wore. Men hated women's tears—her husband had told her so often enough. He'd sneered when he'd told her that women cried for no reason other than to manipulate their menfolk. How could she have been so careless to have let Thorn—*Mr. Dawson*, Daisy reminded herself—see her cry? Would he think she was trying to manipulate him? No, surely not. It wasn't as if Thorn was *hers*, and therefore someone she could persuade to do as she pleased, even if she'd wanted to. And she didn't, of course. Besides, what could she even ask of him? All she wanted was for him to recover his health and go on his way, without ruining her reputation in the process.

"Why's my mother crying? *Did you make her cry?*" an angry young voice demanded.

Neither of them had heard Billy Joe come into the barn. Her face flooding with guilty heat, Daisy flinched away from Thorn as if her son had caught them in an embrace, although naturally nothing could have been further from the truth.

"He he didn't make me cry," Daisy said, her heart pounding at the fury she saw in her son's eyes. While she was grateful that her son was protective of her, the last thing she wanted was for him to get in the habit of responding to every problem with anger, the way his father had. She spoke quickly and tried to keep her voice steady. "We were just… I was telling him about your father…"

"Oh." Billy Joe's shoulders sagged and the hot suspicion in his eyes cooled and was replaced by shame—the shame of a child who had never managed to please a demanding, always-angry parent. Daisy saw her son shoot a glance full of apology at Thorn.

She felt a rush of pity that a boy should have to understand that his father hadn't been worthy of the role, and that his death had been a mercy to Billy Joe and herself, rather than a tragedy.

I'm sorry, son, I should have chosen better.

"I wish you didn't have to go back to the restaurant this evening, Ma." Billy Joe's face was wistful now. "She works too hard, since Pa ain't here no more," he said, as if Thorn needed that explanation.

She saw the man nod with understanding. "I'm sorry, too, son," she murmured. "But if I don't work evenings, Mr. Prendergast will never let me off for church on Sunday mornings. As it is I'm only off duty at the restaurant every other Sunday morning," she added to Thorn. "Tilly, the waitress, gets to be the cook then, and Mr. Prendergast's sister takes over as waitress."

"I dunno why we have go to church, anyway," Billy Joe groused. "Gettin' dressed up just to have to sit still for an hour…"

Daisy tamped down a rush of irritation. Though he had seemed, while they were courting, to be a faithful Christian, once they were married Billy Joe's father had always complained about going to church, too, and in his last few years alive, he'd refused to go at all. "'Trust in the Lord with all thine heart, and lean not unto thine own understanding,'—that's what the Scriptures say. We go because we're God-fearing people, not heathens," Daisy said stiffly. "It's my responsibility to see you get raised properly, which means attending worship service on Sundays. And remember, you agreed not to complain about it if I let Mr. Dawson recover here," she said, with a meaningful glance at Thorn. "Besides," she added, forcing a smile, "don't you remember Reverend Gil saying he always likes hearing you singing the hymns? Maybe you'll sing in the choir when you get older."

Billy Joe snorted as if to demonstrate the likelihood of that.

Daisy cast a guilty look at the light coming into the barn and jumped to her feet.

"Land sakes, how long have we been chattering?" She'd have to go in and check the clock—one of the few household items she'd managed to avoid selling. "I have to get back to the restaurant! I'd planned to get the potatoes peeled so Billy Joe could start cooking them for dinner, to go with the ham that's left."

"I apologize for keeping you from your chores, ma'am," Thorn said politely, rising in turn, with much less ease. "I reckon Billy Joe can peel some potatoes, can't you?" he said, looking to Billy Joe for confirmation.

"'Course I can," the boy muttered.

"All right then, thanks. I'd better scurry," Daisy said. She wasn't entirely sorry that she had to leave, though, to be honest with herself. The truth was, she'd enjoyed time spent speaking with another adult, an adult male at that, in a way that went beyond the brief hellos that were all she could manage when her friends came to eat at the hotel. She couldn't remember when the time had flown so fast. But she shouldn't get used to it, she reminded herself, because he wouldn't be staying.

"Billy Joe, you be careful with that knife, mind. I

need you to start those potatoes, and bring in some kindling. Set the table, too. Right now, or you'll forget." Plus, it would get her chatterbox of a son out of the barn. She'd seen the weariness on Thorn's face and sensed he needed to rest.

"Aww, Ma, do I *have* to?" Billy Joe cried, dragging his foot through a pile of straw. "I was gonna talk to Mr. Thorn and keep him company."

"Billy Joe, a man does what a lady asks of him, especially when that lady is his ma," Thorn said, with a nod of encouragement at the boy. "I was feeling a need for a little nap, anyway."

Was it her imagination, or was Thorn looking a little flushed? "You can come talk to Mr. Dawson after supper—*if* you wash the dishes," Daisy told him. "They'd better be done when I come home."

"Yes, Ma."

Satisfied, Daisy shifted her gaze to Thorn. "Billy Joe will bring out your supper. I'll bid you goodnight now, since it will be late by the time I'm back. Come on, son."

"Thank you, ma'am."

Thorn watched Daisy and the boy go, appreciating the gentle, graceful sway of her skirt as she walked. And because of how much he appreciated that, and how he immediately missed her company as soon as the barn door closed behind her, Thorn knew he needed to get himself gone from here as soon as possible. There was no use becoming too attached to what he couldn't have. Ace was growing restless, too, not being used to spending so much time in a stall. Unfortunately, even though the horse wasn't getting his usual exercise, he was still eating just as much as ever. Thorn couldn't help but feel guilty about the bales of hay and the large bucket of oats that had appeared in the barn shortly after his arrival. He guessed Daisy could ill afford to feed his horse, if she worried about the cost of replacing chicken feed.

Thorn had considered letting the horse out to run off some of that energy. But allowing Ace to exercise in the small pasture behind the barn might have aroused too much curiosity from Daisy's neighbors, since she apparently hadn't had a horse for some time. And if one of the outlaws spotted Thorn's distinctive bay, it would be as good as posting a sign to tell the Griggs gang where he could be found.

If he was going to leave, though, he'd have to regain his strength, which couldn't be done by lying around in a barn all day. He'd have to find some tasks to help make himself active and strong again. For one thing, he'd promised Daisy he'd fix the barn roof before he departed, despite the fact that she'd said it wasn't necessary. He'd have to ponder a way to manage that without being seen.

Right now, though, he was going to sleep. It seemed so hot in the barn all of a sudden. He wished he'd asked the boy to fetch him some cold water before he left him alone...

Some time later, Thorn roused from his sleep wishing he had a blanket. It was so cold his teeth were chattering. *Had a norther blown in while he was napping?*

He must have dozed again, for the lantern Billy Joe had brought was an island of light in the dark barn. The chill had faded completely and Thorn felt scorched with heat again. The boy was shaking him awake. "Thorn! Mr. Dawson! Wake up! Why are you so hot?"

"Billy Joe, is Mr. Dawson all right? Does he want some supper?" he heard Daisy call.

"Ma, he's hot as a firecracker! I cain't hardly wake him!" Billy Joe's voice held an edge of panic.

Knowing Daisy was home brought Thorn partially out of his stupor. He heard her steps quicken, and then she was there, her cool hand to his forehead, her eyes wide with worry. He leaned into her touch, enjoying the coolness.

"Oh, dear, Billy Joe, he's burning up with fever! How long has he been like this? Why didn't you come get me at the restaurant?" she cried.

Thorn raised heavy eyes that wanted to remain shut to the boy hovering nearby and saw him flinch at the worried scolding in her tone.

"I didn't know, Ma," Billy Joe told her. "He was sleeping when I came out to check on him a while ago, but I didn't think nothing about it—you said he'd be sleeping a lot. I didn't think to check for fever… Is he sick, Ma? Is he gonna…" Billy Joe's voice trailed off, but Thorn could fill in what he hadn't said.

"Billy Joe, run and get the doctor, and tell him Mr. Dawson has taken a turn for the worse. Tell him I think his wounds got infected. Hurry now—don't stop for anything!"

"I'll be all right…" Thorn protested, as the boy's running footsteps died away down the street. He staggered to his feet as if to prove what he said. He barely managed to stay upright. "Just have to rest… sweat this out…" He was not altogether sure his idea of a remedy would work, but he didn't want to worry her. The stall was spinning around him and he closed his eyes against the too-bright, flickering light of the lantern. "But have to lie down now…"

He might have collapsed if she hadn't assisted him back onto the cot.

"I'm going to the kitchen to make you some willow-bark tea to get that fever down," she said, and her voice rang loudly in his ears, even though he could tell she had only murmured the words.

The ice was creeping through his veins again. "Bring me a blanket…please…when you come back…"

Chapter Five

"Must be s-some mistake here, Miss Lucybelle. I ordered…wh-whiskey… didn't I?" Thorn mumbled, when Daisy returned and held the cup of warm liquid to his lips. The teeth of his upper jaw rattled against the crockery mug as a chill shook him, and the eyes that stared at her were wide, unfocused and overbright.

He's delirious, she realized. *Oh, when will Dr. Walker get here? What if the fever goes so high that he has a convulsion? What will I do then? Oh, Lord, help me!*

"Drink this," she ordered, in a firm but kind voice. "You're sick, Thorn, and we need to get your fever down. And I'm Daisy, not Lucybelle. Do you know where you are?"

He looked around him with reddened, bleary eyes and wiped his sweaty forehead on his shirt-sleeve. "No," he admitted. "But wh-wherever it is, it's mighty hot—then sometimes cold as a blue norther. H-how's it changing like that? You—you're not Lucybelle? No, I… Now that I'm lookin', I—I guess I see that you ain't. You got…light…h-hair like her, but hers is more y-yaller—*yellow* than yours is, I reckon," he corrected himself, as if he realized how slurred his speech was.

"No, I'm Daisy Henderson, and you're in my barn here in Simpson Creek, Texas. You're recovering from gunshot wounds, and you got feverish—that's why you thought I was someone else."

"Daisy…" he said, reaching out a shaking hand and cupping her cheek. "You're p-purtier than Lucybelle…but not's purty as Selena. Don't you t-try to t-tempt me. Cain't s-stay here. Got to get back…to S-Selena."

Lucybelle had sounded like a saloon girl, since he was expecting her to bring whiskey. But who was Selena? Another saloon girl, perhaps? It seemed there were several women in Thorn's life, Daisy thought.

"I'm not trying to tempt you, Thorn," she said agreeably. "I'm trying to get you well, so you can go back to Selena…or Lucybelle, as you wish. So drink the tea, so we can get that fever down. Then, once you're recovered, you can figure out where you want to go."

That was apparently enough motivation, for Thorn took hold of the cup and swallowed the rest of the liquid. The face he made afterward would have been comical if the situation wasn't so dire.

"Whew! B-bitter st-stuff…" he muttered. "R-rotgut. Haven't you got any g-good whiskey, Lucybelle?"

"Afraid not," Daisy said, realizing that it was useless to insist this was medicine, or to try to convince him to call her by the correct name right now. Even though he seemed to be able to hear her, the meaning behind her words wasn't really getting through the haze of the fever. "But you drank it, and that's good. You don't have to pay for it since you didn't like it, Thorn," she added, when he reached into the pocket of his trousers as if fishing for coins.

"Okay…thass—*that's*—mighty kind 'a you…" He frowned, clearly thinking. "It won't get you in trouble though, will it?"

"No, of course not. Don't worry about that."

"Lemme have th' blanket, Lucybelle…cold in here. Musta had a n-norther blow in…"

Daisy spread the blanket around his shivering shoulders, then dipped the cloth she'd brought into the bucket of cool water and began to sponge his forehead. But he was apparently too much in the throes of his chill, for he pushed the damp cloth away.

"No-o-o, t-too cold… Why are ya tryin' t' freeze me, w-woman?"

"Thorn, we have to get the fever down—"

But it was no use trying to reason with a man who was out of his head with delirium. When he continued to struggle against her, she sank back on her heels, afraid he would strike out at her in his confusion.

Then she heard the pounding of footsteps outside, and a moment later Dr. Walker burst into the stall, panting, with Billy Joe close at his heels. *Thank You, God.*

Both the doctor and the boy were as red-faced as Thorn. Bless their hearts, they had apparently run all the way from the other end of town.

Dr. Walker let his bag drop into the hay with a thud and worked to catch his breath as Daisy told him how they'd found Thorn feverish, then freezing. How he'd begun talking out of his head, and that she'd given him some willow-bark tea.

"Good, good," Nolan Walker muttered in approval. He pulled Thorn's shirt up and lifted the edge of the bandage to peer at his shoulder wound, then checked the graze on his leg. Daisy told Billy Joe to go to bed, and for once, thankfully, he did so without argument.

"His leg seems fine, but the wound in the shoulder is infected, right enough. I'd worried about that one—it's a bad wound, and he went quite a few hours before treatment. Still, I see no sign of gangrene," Dr. Walker said, after the barn door closed behind the boy. "So he's got a chance…"

"A chance?" Daisy repeated, full of fear at the grim look in the doctor's eyes.

He nodded. "It could go either way. He's going to need a lot of nursing and prayer, but with both of those, there's a chance that he could survive."

She thought then that the doctor would insist on moving Thorn out of the barn and down to his house, where he had a two-bed infirmary, but he didn't. "First, we've got to get that fever down," the doctor said.

He administered laudanum to sedate Thorn, who was still thrashing on the cot, and at last the wounded man lay quietly, not struggling against the cool wet cloths they wiped him down with. They worked on his body section by section, keeping the rest of him covered to battle against the chill that had him shivering from head to toe. They tended him for hours, fighting against the fever, coaxing him into choking down more tea, and quietly praying together.

At last Dr. Walker, after feeling his forehead with a practiced hand, announced that the fever had broken.

"So he'll live?" Daisy asked. "Thank You, God—"

Walker held up a palm as if to stop her flood of gratitude. "I'm sorry, but he's not out of the woods yet, Miss Daisy. The fever's down for now, but it'll go back up again. Perhaps I'd better move him down to my office. It's going to take a lot of vigilance—"

"No, please, leave him here," she begged, though

she wasn't sure why she said it. How was she going to keep nursing him *and* do her job? If he was moved to the infirmary, he'd be able to get better and more constant care. Plus he'd be out of her hands, no longer able to cause her disgrace. She told herself she was objecting because if they moved him now, the commotion might cause her nosy neighbor, Mrs. Donahue, to peek out of her window and realize that Daisy had been harboring a man in her barn. And since the doctor was there, too, and Mrs. Donahue might have seen the sheriff going into the barn earlier, it wouldn't take the woman long to put two and two together and realize it was one of the bank robbers.

Daisy admitted to herself there was another reason she had to be the one to nurse Thorn Dawson back to health—because of Peter. She hadn't been able to save her brother, so she had to succeed with Thorn, despite all the limitations on her time that she hadn't had then.

"I want to keep him here. We'll do whatever has to be done," she told the doctor.

There must have been something about the uncompromising firmness of her tone that said she would not budge on this point, for he finally nodded his acquiescence. Or did the doctor choose not to argue because he thought it didn't matter much if an outlaw who claimed he wasn't an outlaw died of his wounds? She didn't dare ask.

"Very well," Dr. Walker said, "though I can't

think you realize what you're getting into. I want you to know you can change your mind at any time, Miss Daisy. Here's what you're going to need to do…"

She listened carefully as he went over the details of treating Dawson's fever if it went back up, keeping him on a simple diet that he could manage even in his stupor, changing his dressings.

"I'll leave a little laudanum with you in case his pain gets worse," Dr. Walker added, handing her a small amber bottle. "Be very careful in measuring out the amount. A teaspoon, no more, and only if his pain is bad. Too much could kill him. And if he gets too used to it, he won't be able to do without it."

She nodded, but she doubted Thorn would be asking for it. He seemed the sort of man to tough it out, rather than use laudanum as a crutch.

"I'll come by every day to check on him, but if you need me to return sooner, just send Billy Joe down to get me as you did tonight."

Then he was gone.

Daisy stared down at Thorn, who now lay fast asleep, his skin no longer flushed with fever, his chest rising and falling easily. She'd better get Billy Joe settled for the night, too, then return here to sit with Thorn. She hoped her son would go to sleep quickly tonight and would not pester her with questions, so he wouldn't have to know his mother would be spending her night keeping vigil over the sick man. She knew that her son would offer to perform the vigil himself, and there was no way she could turn that responsibility over to Billy Joe, especially while there was still a chance that Thorn could die, despite all their care.

Lord, please raise Thorn Dawson back up to health, she prayed as she finally sat down in her kitchen to eat her supper. *I prayed for You to save Peter, and I don't know why Your answer was no then, though I'm sure You had Your reasons. But I fear watching another man die would shatter me, and I fear what it might do to Billy Joe.*

Billy Joe had gone to bed as she'd instructed, and when she'd looked in on him after washing the dishes, he was asleep in the complete way that only the young and innocent can manage. He'd looked much younger than he was—as young as Peter had been when he'd cut himself with an ax while chopping wood.

Their parents had been away at a camp meeting, a religious revival held at intervals in their locale. As devoted as everyone was to their local church, a camp meeting was a special occasion—a chance to really focus on faith for days at a time, away from all other concerns. People came from miles around and camped out to hear the Word preached, to sing and have fellowship with other believers around the campfire while they shared their provisions. It was as much a social outlet as a religious experience, one of the few such outlets her strict parents allowed themselves. Daisy had been to other camp meetings, but this time she was to stay home and watch out for her brother, who wasn't going because he needed to stay and tend their stock.

It hadn't been a big cut on his leg that Peter had suffered when the ax slipped, and after coming inside to get a rag to bandage it with, he'd gone back to chopping wood, promising her that he'd wash the wound properly with soap and water once he had replenished the wood she'd need for cooking. She'd gotten busy with meal preparation and cleanup when the meal was done, leaving the kitchen neat as a pin, and hadn't thought to remind him, or to check that he'd tended the wound properly. Now, years later, she was pretty sure that Peter had never washed the wound the way that he'd promised he would.

Within a day or so he was feverish and ill, and red streaks had spread upward from the wound. There was no doctor in their little settlement back then; the nearest one living some twenty miles away, and she couldn't ride to fetch him because their parents had taken both their horses to pull the buckboard they'd driven to the camp meeting. She'd called in the neighbors, the few who hadn't gone to the revival, but all they did was look frightened and twist their aprons as Peter got sicker and more delirious and the leg turned greenish-black. Finally, one of them sent for her parents, but it was too late; despite all her prayers and pleadings with God, Peter had died just an hour before their parents reached home.

They'd never said so out loud, but Daisy knew they'd always secretly blamed her for failing to save their only son.

So please, Lord, she prayed as she gathered up blankets and fresh sheets to take out to the barn with her, *have mercy on Thorn Dawson, and on Billy Joe and me, and let Mr. Dawson live. I cannot imagine what Dawson dying would do to Billy Joe. I wouldn't want him to stop believing in You, as I did for so long after Peter died. And I'm afraid failing again—this time to save this man's life—would shatter me. I need to stay strong for Billy Joe's sake, so he can grow up a strong, good man and follow Your paths, not take on the evil ways of his father.*

In the barn, Daisy found her patient still asleep, and his forehead was still cool and dry. But it was not the peaceful, restorative sleep that her son was experiencing inside the house. Every few seconds, Thorn thrashed and twisted on the bed, his face contorted as if he found no solace in his slumber.

It's the laudanum, she thought. It relieved pain, but the doctor had told her it could cause vivid, horrible dreams—a good thing, in Dr. Walker's opinion, or more men would be addicted to its powerful influence than there were.

"Selena…" he moaned, an hour later, startling Daisy from her dozing.

Who *was* Selena? she wondered again. For him to call for her so often, she must be very close to his heart. Did Thorn Dawson have a sweetheart? Or was he perhaps a married man, leaving a wife alone somewhere, wondering if he was alive or dead? As soon as he was lucid, Daisy would have to find out. Then she would write this Selena and let her know her husband—or sweetheart—was being cared for to the best of Daisy's ability. Perhaps Selena would even come and take him home.

Daisy tried to imagine what the woman looked like. Judging by her name, she sounded like a *Tejana*, a Mexican Texan, and Daisy pictured her with dark, flashing eyes, hair the color of a raven's wing, with a ready, husky laugh and vivacious personality. Her complete opposite, both in coloring and temperament.

Selena. She'd been the reason he'd stayed in Texas when war broke out, instead of joining the army and going to fight with Hood, as so many of his friends had. Anyway, Thorn couldn't see the point in leaving to fight the northern half of these United States for the right to own other people, when he didn't own any slaves and never wanted to. He'd seen the danger in all the men going off, too, since if they all left their wives and sweethearts, it was as good as issuing an invitation to the Comanches and Kiowas and lawless white renegades to come and attack as much as they pleased, taking whatever they wanted and leaving nothing to come home to when the war was over. So he'd signed on with the Texas Rangers and fought with them to protect the state, while the other men went to fight the Yankees. Of course, working with the Rangers had had its share of dangers, but at least he was still there in Texas, could still see Selena often and make sure she was safe.

But she had died, anyway, caught in a vicious ambush purely by chance when she rode to meet Thorn for a picnic on the Llano River. He'd been late to arrive, for he'd bought her a ring at the mercantile, intending to propose marriage, and thought it only fitting to present it along with a bouquet of Indian paintbrush that grew in a field about a mile away. While he'd been picking flowers, Selena had been attacked at the riverbank by a roving gang who thought the lone woman easy prey. No doubt they'd planned to make a slave of her and sell her to the highest bidder after violating her, but she'd apparently resisted to the point where they had decided it would be easier to stab her and leave her dying, for him to find moments before she took her last breath. She'd never known he'd planned for this to be the happiest day of her life.

Now in his delirium she floated above him, looking just as she had when he'd found her that tragic day—pallid as a bleached bone except for the crimson slashes of her wounds, reaching for him desperately, longingly, her dark eyes huge in her too-white face.

"Selena…" *Come back. Give me another chance to save you, to protect you. I'll never leave your side again…*

He heard another female voice, and saw a woman bending over him, her face full of worry. Her hair and eyes were as pale as Selena's had been dark, and she was pretty, though in a way that revealed she had known much care in her life, where Selena's had been carefree until that fateful day.

The fair-haired woman spoke now, and he had trouble understanding her words because of the hot swirling, choking fog that surrounded him. But he thought she said, "I'm not Selena, I'm Daisy, and you have to fight this, Thorn, *fight*. You have to *live*."

He couldn't see the point, honestly. If he gave in to the fever that burned like an inferno within him, he'd be with Selena, and he knew he could be happy wherever she was. But the woman just kept sponging him with that cold, cold water, no matter how much he tried to protest and push her away, so he doubted he'd get his druthers.

Chapter Six

Two days later, Thorn woke from his feverish delirium, clear of mind but weak as a day-old calf. Every joint and muscle ached. His mouth was dry as the middle of a dust storm. He felt like a washcloth that had been wrung dry of every drop of water it had held. When he managed to focus his eyes, he made out the figure of Billy Joe, not Daisy, sitting on the hay bale beside his cot. Had Thorn only dreamed that she'd been there by his side every time he'd wakened while the fever held?

"W-water," he croaked, startling Billy Joe so badly that the boy nearly fell off the bale.

"You—you're awake," the boy breathed, eyes goggling as if he could hardly believe it.

"Yes…th-thirsty… Need water…"

Billy Joe jumped to his feet and went to another hay bale, where a pitcher was sitting, and poured a small amount of water in a tin cup. This he held to Thorn's lips, murmuring, "Take it slow, now. Don't try to drink it fast or you'll choke."

The first few swallows didn't reach their destination, for Thorn's throat was so parched all he could do was cough and sputter, not swallow, bringing him no relief. But once he realized that the boy was right and he'd have to sip, not take big drafts, he was more successful, and the water finally cooled his mouth and reached his gullet. He could practically feel himself coming alive again. He drank the entire glass as slowly as he could force himself to take it.

"Wh-where's D-Daisy?" he asked, when the boy told him he'd have to wait a bit before drinking any more.

Billy Joe stared at him. "Ma's sleeping, and I'm not going to wake her," he said, his chin jutting forward a bit pugnaciously. "She's about dead on her feet after three days of working all day and watching over you all night. I told her to go to bed, that I'd watch out for you tonight, but she only agreed to 'cause she said you were getting better."

"S-sorry to make so much trouble," Thorn said, feeling bad that Daisy was exhausted because of him, though he certainly wouldn't have chosen to fall ill as he had. "No, there's no need to wake her. She needs her sleep."

His response must have mollified Billy Joe somewhat, for the boy said, "She left some soup on the stove for you, if you woke up. You want it?"

It seemed to take an enormous effort just to nod, and Thorn wasn't entirely sure he'd succeeded, so he added aloud, "Please. Soup w-would be g-good." Sleepiness was creeping over him, threatening to reclaim him. He hoped he could remain awake long enough to eat the soup, for he knew instinctively that nourishment was the key to getting his strength back. He doubted they'd been able to get much food into him during the course of his fever.

It seemed like only seconds later that the boy was shaking him awake. "I thought you wanted this soup, Mr. Dawson. You gotta wake up." He sounded put out that Thorn had fallen asleep instead of waiting for his return, and Thorn considered that the boy had gone to some trouble to warm the soup, so he roused himself enough to sit up and eat it. It was chicken with vegetables, and he decided he'd never tasted anything better in his life, not even steak. But he only had enough strength to down half a dozen spoonfuls before he felt his eyelids drifting shut again.

"Sorry," he murmured. "I'll eat the rest…later. You…go on to bed, B-Billy Joe."

The boy shook his head, his eyes fierce. "No, sir. Ma said to sit up with you and make sure you didn't need anything, so that's what I'm a-gonna do," he declared.

"No n-need," he told Billy Joe, but he could see it

would do no good to argue, so didn't bother to protest any further. He just let his eyes drift shut again.

As he sank back down onto the cot, he caught a
whiff of himself. One thing was certain—he was
going to ask for some water to wash with as soon as
he was strong enough. He smelled worse than a mil-
dewed saddle blanket. He felt a flash of embarrassment for having let Daisy see—and smell—him in
such a state, but then the drowsiness took over and
everything, even embarrassment, faded away.

"You sure look better than you have in the last
few days," Tilly commented when she arrived at the
hotel restaurant the next morning, close to being late,
as usual.

Her remark caught Daisy by surprise. The waitress usually had nothing nice to say to her, and this
was as close to a compliment as she had ever offered.

Daisy stirred the scrambled eggs cooking in the
huge iron skillet in front of her. "Thank you. I got a
good night's sleep last night, so I feel pretty chipper."
It *had* been restoring to get a solid amount of sleep
in her own bed, knowing her "guest" in the barn was
improving, and Billy Joe was on watch during the
night. It had been even better to go out to the barn
after she'd arisen this morning and find Thorn Dawson sitting up on his cot, eyes alert, his color good,
and his voice strong and steady as he assured her he
was eager to devour breakfast.

He's going to live, her heart had sung within her. She hadn't failed this time. He wasn't going to die, as her brother had.

"Oh, too bad," Tilly said in a disappointed tone. "I thought maybe you'd met someone, and had a gentleman caller visit you last night."

Daisy felt a flush threatening to bloom on her cheeks. Thorn was certainly no "gentleman caller," but the woman had come too close to the truth with her insinuation that there was a new man in Daisy's life. "Where would I meet a beau, Tilly? No, my son is the only man I need or want in my life."

"Don't knock it if you haven't tried it," the waitress said in her sly way. "That son of yours is going to be all growed up and gone someday, and then where will you be? All alone, that's where. I have a beau, and I highly recommend it."

Daisy wondered idly where Tilly had met such a man, then figured it was better not to ask. She knew the other woman flirted tirelessly with cowboys and other bachelors who came in for a meal, and knew too that their boss would fire the waitress if he knew about it, for Mr. Prendergast was a stickler for propriety in his employees. If Daisy was as ruthless as Tilly, she'd tell Mr. Prendergast all about the waitress's behavior…but she couldn't bring herself to do it. Tilly needed this job, just as Daisy needed hers. It would be unkind and unchristian to try to get her dismissed as waitress. And anyway, Daisy wasn't the sort to tattle.

"I'm glad you have a beau, but Billy Joe is my priority," she said, and was relieved when the tinkling bell at the entrance of the restaurant announced their first customer. Tilly would have to turn her attention to business now. Daisy began to think of what she would cook for the noon meal, and of taking it home to Thorn for his lunch during her break.

As she'd been leaving the barn, he had asked Billy Joe to bring him his razor from his saddlebags so he could shave. After checking with Daisy for her approval, Billy Joe had offered to lend him her hand mirror, too. The idea of seeing Thorn clean-shaven and wearing a fresh shirt put a spring in her step that hadn't been there before.

Careful, she told herself. *Don't get too used to his presence. He's no "gentleman caller" like Tilly has been gushing about. Now that Dawson is on the mend, he'll be leaving soon and chances are you'll never see him again.*

Two days had passed since he'd woken after his fever, and although his wounds still pained him some, Thorn wasn't remotely tempted to ask for any more laudanum. Who needed the sort of weird, fantastic dreams the medicine brought on? He was finally feeling "on the mend" as both the sawbones and Daisy had pronounced him to be.

Recovery was making him restless. While he wasn't at all eager to return to the outlaws and their constant plotting about who to steal from next, not to mention the danger involved with those escapades to the outlaws themselves and to their hapless victims, Thorn figured they would have ways of hearing that he hadn't died of his wounds. After all, if he'd died then his body would have turned up by this point. Since it hadn't, they had to be curious about where he was right now.

Before long they'd come looking for him, if they weren't already. No one left the Griggs gang unless Griggs himself wanted you gone—and that usually meant he was sending you straight to your Maker. If the gang figured Thorn was alive then they would find him and bring him back into the fold, whether he wanted to go or not.

And he sure didn't want them to find him here, nursed by the lovely Daisy Henderson. Exposing her to danger would be a poor return for her kindness and care. Just the thought of Gordon Griggs looking at Daisy Henderson made Thorn's blood boil and his fists clench. No, he had to get strong so he could leave and make sure Griggs's and Daisy's paths never intersected.

In any case, he was eager to see his mission finished. And it couldn't be finished till the Griggs gang was behind bars.

He'd been forcing himself to get up and walk the

length of the barn several times that day, and he was feeling stronger as a result of even that little exercise. He'd have liked to step out in the sunlight and fresh air, to see if he was strong enough to walk from one end of the little town to the other, but of course he didn't dare show his face outside. But now, under the cover of darkness, he was eager to feel the night air on his face.

Daisy had just bid him good-night and left. He slipped out of his stall and opened the barn door enough that he could watch the house. He saw a light in one room—Billy Joe's?—and then it was extinguished. Then another window was lit by a lantern. It burned for a few minutes, and he wondered if Daisy was reading. If so, what would she read—her Bible? Thorn felt that he knew a great deal about her character—about the kind of person she was. And yet he knew so little about her tastes and preferences. Was she fond of reading? Did she like novels, or poetry? Did she have a favorite Psalm, or a particular verse she turned to for comfort in times of trouble? He had no idea.

Then that light, too, went out. He saw that she'd left her window open a few inches, no doubt to catch the breeze. She would fall asleep soon. Was there a chance she would dream of him? She had started appearing in his dreams—a sweet and comforting presence that soothed him into peaceful rest. Perhaps he could be a comfort to her in her dreams? Never had he seen a woman so in need of the comfort and reassurance a man could give. If only he could—

No. Thorn forced himself to stop his imaginings. No good could come of such thoughts.

He waited until the house had been still for a while, then slipped out the narrow opening, enjoying the feel of the warm summer night breeze on his skin as he walked around the perimeter of the property, swinging his arms and stretching his muscles. He wished he dared take Ace out for a night run, but it would be too noisy. Even if he was able to avoid the creaking when he pulled the barn door open just far enough to let Ace out, and the chances were high that his horse would whinny in excitement at the prospect of a gallop, which would waken Daisy or the boy. If Thorn was going to risk it, he'd need to make sure that the conditions were just right.

He studied the night sky. Tomorrow the moon would be full, so it would be better to wait till then for his ride. He'd just have to hope he didn't happen to run into members of the Griggs gang, out prowling around looking for mischief. He had no idea where they were hiding out, for Griggs had made no advance plan for a rendezvous spot in case they were scattered after the bank robbery. And they might have done more than one heist since then, which would have caused them to relocate anyway. No, the Griggs gang could be anywhere...so there was no point in trying to avoid them. It wasn't as if he could hide for the rest of his life.

Thorn thought about telling Daisy what he was going to do, so she wouldn't worry if she heard him go out. But no, she'd be concerned that he was over-extending himself so soon after his infection and fever.

Worry? She won't worry, he told himself. She probably couldn't wait to be shed of him and the chance of scandal he represented. It would be too bad if she was shamed again because of a man— and this time one she hadn't even chosen for herself.

Feeling pleasantly tired, but stronger than he had since the day of the bank robbery, he returned to the barn, hoping the fresh air he'd gotten would put him quickly to sleep, so he wouldn't think of Daisy. But he lay awake till early dawn, his mind awash with thoughts of her.

The next night, after all was quiet in the house again, Thorn stuck to his plan of taking Ace out for a ride. He was careful to walk the horse onto Main Street and a good ways beyond Daisy's house before he mounted. He reached the far edge of town before he let the gelding have his head and accelerate to a full gallop, always watching in the moonlight for any hazards in the road ahead. He reveled in the smooth play of the gelding's muscles beneath him, and it seemed that Ace savored the wind whistling through his mane as his hooves ate up the road. He felt that the gelding was still eager to run when Thorn reined him back toward town and forced him into a walk, but he was too good a horseman to return a lathered animal to his stall without a proper cooling down. Nearing the Henderson house again, he was careful to dismount and lead the horse back into the barn, moving as quietly as possible to reduce the chance of a neighbor hearing him and Acc pass by. No flares of light illumined any windows inside the Henderson house, so it seemed he had not been missed.

Both of his wounds stung from the unaccustomed exercise as he unsaddled his horse and put him back in the stall Ace had been occupying, but Thorn doubted he'd set his healing back any by his ride. It was a good hurt—the kind that came from hard work that left you stronger for having done it. If he kept exercising each day, soon he'd be fit enough to climb up onto the barn roof and repair that hole. When he'd finally explored the barn fully, he'd found a ladder in the tack room tall enough to get him up there, along with a pile of cedar shakes and a sack of nails, as if at some point the late Mr. Henderson had intended to repair his roof, before his untimely death. But if he had the materials, then why had he waited?

What sort of man shirked his duty to his home and family instead of taking care of his property? Silly question, Thorn told himself as he lay down to sleep. William Wilbur Henderson had obviously not been any sort of responsible family man. Daisy and Billy Joe deserved better, and Thorn hoped and prayed that they would find it someday—in the future, when he was long gone and wouldn't have to see it happen.

"Where did you go last night?" Daisy asked him when she brought his meal at midday. She'd debated asking him this question all morning, while she worked. He might say that it wasn't any of her business, but she had to at least try to ask.

His face took on a sheepish look. "I'm sorry if I disturbed you. I tried to be quiet," Thorn said. "My horse was getting a mite fidgety from lack of exercise, so I took him out for a ride."

"Oh, I didn't hear you, Billy Joe did." Her son had come to her room, his face stricken. "He…he was afraid you were leaving us without saying goodbye."

"I wouldn't do that," Thorn told her. "It'd be a poor return on your kindness for letting me recuperate here." Of course, his departure was inevitable. He'd have to leave someday. But it was a relief to hear that he wasn't intending to leave them just yet.

"I didn't believe you'd sneak away like that, either— and I told him so." She wouldn't tell Thorn how Billy Joe had lain awake, fretting—and she had, too, not only because her son was upset, but because the idea distressed her—until they'd heard him return. "Did you meet up with your outlaw friends while you were out?"

He gave a wry smile and shook his head. "The Griggs gang is probably on the other side of the Rio Grande by now, if they're smart." At least he hoped they were. "No, Ace and I didn't encounter a soul out there, just a mule deer and a jackrabbit out for a stroll. But it was good to get out of this barn for a while."

"You didn't overdo it, did you? Doc Walker won't thank you for aggravating your wounds."

"I'm feeling better every day," he assured her.

She'd probably sounded silly, fussing over him like that. She'd seem like a nagging wife—something Thorn surely wouldn't appreciate. Unless he had a wife already? She never had asked him about that Selena he'd mentioned when he'd been delirious. But if he had a wife to fuss over him already, then he'd appreciate her nagging even less. "Th-that's good… Where *is* Billy Joe, by the way? I'm surprised he's not out here bothering you."

"He's no bother," Thorn told her. "He brought me the breakfast you left for me—thank you kindly for that, Miss Daisy. Then I heard some of his friends come and invite him to go fishing at the creek with them." He shrugged. "The boy's probably getting tired of my stories."

She gave a skeptical laugh. "I doubt it. But it's hard to compete with the lure of the creek on a hot

June day. Don't count on fish for supper, though—they rarely catch much, because they end up swimming more than fishing. Even when they try I think they end up making so much noise they scare all the fish away."

Thorn smiled wryly. "Too bad. I was already tasting fried fillets. If you cook fish as well as everything else, it'd be tasty."

She was so warmed by the unexpected compliment, she had to look away. "Thank you, Mr. Dawson."

"Reckon you could see your way clear to calling me Thorn?" he asked. "We've been acquainted for quite a spell now…"

Still not meeting his gaze, she murmured, "I suppose so…when no one else is around…"

I shouldn't have agreed to that, she thought, *nor made that additional remark that implied a certain intimacy when it was just the two of us. I'd only meant to indicate I wouldn't do it in front of Billy Joe, because it wouldn't be proper. What would my son think if he heard his mother calling our unlikely guest by his Christian name? And what is it about this man that makes me abandon common sense?*

Perhaps Thorn sensed her discomfort, for he started speaking again. "When I was a boy, I used to play hooky from my chores and fish in a creek that ran through our ranch. As I recall, I did more swimming than fishing then, too. The fish wouldn't bite on a hot day, anyway." His chuckle made her smile, too, and relax, at least a little bit.

It was time to get back to work. Tilly had made another of her snide remarks just this morning about Billy Joe, and Daisy's supposed need to rush back to the house lately so she could be constantly checking up on him, so she dared not give the waitress any more reason to be nosy.

"That was a mighty big sigh," Thorn commented, when she'd stood up. "Is your boss giving you a hard time?"

She hadn't realized she had sighed out loud. "No, Mr. Prendergast mostly keeps his nose out of the kitchen, unless there's a problem. It's just that Tilly, the waitress, would really like my job, so she never misses a chance to try to make me look bad. She's mighty curious about why I'm suddenly checking up on Billy Joe so much during my break time."

Thorn seemed to tense slightly. "Then I reckon you better stop coming home on your breaks," he said.

His tone was so unwontedly sharp that she realized a nosy Tilly could be a danger to him if she came to check up on Daisy. The waitress had never come to her house before, but Daisy wouldn't put anything past the girl if she thought there was some advantage to gain. Daisy had been so worried about safeguarding her own reputation that she had for-

gotten Thorn had the threat of jail or even hanging
awaiting him if his presence was discovered.

"But you have to have something to eat," she
protested, knowing he was right, but aware that she
would miss these stolen moments of his company.
"It's not as if Billy Joe could fix you an actual meal."

"He can fix me a snack well enough, and as for a
proper meal, it won't hurt me to wait to eat till suppertime," Thorn told her. "And you don't need to
be skipping meals by giving them to me, either," he
added, sending her a meaningful look. "A good gust
of wind would blow you away as it is, Miss Daisy."

She knew she was too thin. *Did Thorn think she
looked scrawny? And if he did, why should she care?*

Regardless, she couldn't dillydally any longer.
"I'd better go. I'll check on you after work," she told
him, and left the barn.

The afternoon seemed endless, with nothing more
to do than wish the time would go by faster so he
could see Daisy again. Thorn realized he was becoming quite attached to the woman in whose barn he
had taken refuge. Attached? No, that was too tame
a word for what he was starting to feel. He thought
he could very easily fall in love with her.

He imagined being able to marry her and whisk
her and the boy away from Simpson Creek. They
could settle on his ranch near Mason, and she'd never
have to work so hard for a living again. There the

only meals she would need to cook would be for the three of them, and Thorn would show her his appreciation for each and every delicious bite. Lord willing, there would be other little mouths to feed around the table in time, and he'd thank God every day for finding her barn when he'd thought he was dying.

If she was his wife, he'd resign from the State Police and make his living as a rancher. It was hard work, and the cattle could be just as ornery as outlaws some days, but it wasn't likely any of the cows would start shooting at him. And Daisy could forget about silly young women like the one who thought tattling her way into the cook's job was the pinnacle of success.

But he was fooling himself to even consider such a future. Without the reward money he could earn from bringing the Griggs gang to justice, he would have no funds to start his new life as a rancher. No cash meant he couldn't buy cattle. The cattle already on the ranch properly belonged to his sister and brother-in-law, as they were the ones who had raised and tended the cattle for all these years. Taking the herd as his own would be unfair—but purchasing a new herd wouldn't come cheaply. Daisy's life would be just as hardscrabble as before.

How could she respect him then, let alone love him? How could she even consider accepting him when he had so little to offer?

The barn door was thrown back so hard it slammed

against the wall next to it. Thorn dived for the pistol he'd hidden in the hay once Daisy had given it back to him, and was poised against the side of the stall, ready for whatever was coming, when Billy Joe cried out, "Mr. Thorn, Mr. Thorn! Wait'll you see what I got for us!"

With a sigh of relief at the false alarm, Thorn shoved the pistol back into the hay in the far corner of the stall, then put his finger to his lips as the boy came bursting into the stall. "I reckon a body could hear you clear to San Saba, Billy Joe. You want to give away my hideout location?" He kept his tone mild, not wanting to stifle the boy's enthusiasm, but Daisy had told him about nosy Mrs. Donahue next door, and he didn't want the woman to overhear.

Billy Joe clapped a hand to his mouth. "Sorry, Mr. Thorn. Guess I forgot."

"So, did you catch a mess of bluegills?" Thorn asked, looking over the boy's shoulder as if a stringer loaded with freshly-caught fish might be hidden there, instead of the canvas poke he could see. But his nose was already hinting at what the lad had brought, and it sure wasn't anything Billy Joe could have caught at the end of a fishing line.

"Nope, I caught *this!*" Billy Joe proclaimed, reaching into the sack and bringing out a pie—peach, by the smell of it, Thorn thought. "One of Miss Ella's pies, fresh outta the oven at the café!"

It was a beauty of a pie, perfectly browned, and

its savory smell hinted at how good it would taste. Thorn remembered seeing the sign for the café at the eastern edge of town the day the gang had ridden into Simpson Creek. It seemed to be a competitor for the hotel restaurant where Daisy worked. "And how did you happen to come by that?" he inquired.

Billy Joe stood up even straighter than he had before, obviously proud of himself. "I sneaked up on it stealthy as a Comanche."

Thorn raised an eyebrow. "What do you mean?" But he was afraid he already knew.

Billy Joe grinned. "It was coolin' on the back windowsill at the café, fresh outta the oven. One of my pals told me he didn't think I could snatch it without Miss Ella or her helper catchin' me. If I proved him wrong, I got to keep the whole pie and didn't have to share it with the rest of the boys."

"And if you lost?" Thorn asked grimly.

"Then I would've had to do whatever Miss Ella made me do. But she never saw me and I got clean away, slick as any outlaw."

"What if you hadn't gotten away?" Thorn asked him, his voice stern. "What if Miss Ella had caught you?"

"Oh, she'd probably just make me wash dishes or somethin'," Billy Joe said, his tone careless. But Thorn could tell he was beginning to sense his listener's disapproval. "She's a nice lady."

"And do you think that's the way you should treat

nice ladies—stealing from them when they've never done you any harm?" Billy Joe was starting to look a little embarrassed, so Thorn pressed the point.

"Your ma's a mighty nice lady. How would you like it if someone used that as a reason why it would be all right to steal from her?"

"I wouldn't let nobody steal from my ma!" Billy Joe protested, indignant.

"You'd be real angry if someone tried to, wouldn't you?"

"'Course I would!"

"Then why do you think it's fine and dandy to steal from a nice lady like Miss Ella?"

Billy Joe seemed to be pondering this, so Thorn let him think undisturbed, hoping he was finally realizing that what he'd done was wrong.

"So…" the boy said thoughtfully a minute later, "I shouldn't rob nice people, just mean people, instead? Is that what you do, Mr. Thorn?"

Thorn sighed. Apparently the message hadn't quite gotten through, after all.

"No, Billy Joe. It's never right to steal. You've got no right to take something that you know belongs to someone else."

"But if the person ain't nice to others then they don't deserve to have folks be nice to them, right? I don't gotta be all that sorry when bad things happen to bad people, do I?"

Thorn bit back a sigh. Had he been this much of

a handful when he was Billy Joe's age? He wanted to believe the answer was no, but he had no doubt that his sisters would say he had been a handful and a half. And there had been five of them to keep an eye on him—Billy Joe's mother was all on her own, and working herself to the bone while raising her son, to boot.

"Look at it this way," he suggested. "You weren't worried about Miss Ella making you do anything real bad even if she caught you taking the pie, because she's a nice lady. But if you'd stolen from someone who wasn't so nice and gotten caught, that person might have summoned the sheriff. Then Sheriff Bishop would have marched you off to a cell in his jail and charged you with theft. What would your mama have said to that? Do you think she'd be proud of her outlaw son?"

Billy Joe's head sank on his chest as if he suddenly couldn't hold it up anymore. "I reckon not…" he murmured. "Okay, I won't steal no more food," he said. "But we might as well enjoy the pie, now that I got it."

"I don't think so," Thorn said. "I think you need to escort that pie back to Miss Ella's café, and take whatever punishment she wants to dish out—unless you've got money to pay her for it, that is."

"I ain't got any money. And I ain't gonna take it back," he insisted, a stubborn look coming over his features. "The boys might see me, and they'd laugh at me."

"So you care more about what your friends think than about doing what you know is right?"

Billy Joe dropped his gaze to his dusty shoes. "I—I guess not," he mumbled. "Aw, Mr. Thorn, do I *hafta* take it back?"

"Do you think *I* should take it back for you?"

Thorn could see Billy Joe would have liked to take advantage of his offer, but knew he couldn't.

"Thanks, but someone might see you and recognize you as one of the robbers. 'Sides, you weren't the one who took it. But Mr. Thorn, what if Miss Ella tells Ma what I done?"

"Is taking it back the right thing to do, no matter what Miss Ella does?"

Billy Joe let out a gusty sigh. "I… I reckon so." The boy took a last regretful look at the pie, then put it back in his poke. "I'll be back soon as I can," he said, squaring his shoulders, then walking out of the barn.

Thorn watched him go. The pie would have been a treat, but he hoped he'd helped the boy begin to change his attitude about outlawing and stealing. If so, maybe it was a start at paying back Daisy for all she'd done for him.

With supper done, and Billy Joe taking a much-needed bath, Daisy arranged a plate of food to take out to Thorn. She was tired from work, but eager to see him, especially after what her son had told her of the day's events.

She saw that Thorn had done some cleaning up while she'd been gone—he had shaved and there was a cake of soap and a damp towel in the corner of the stall, as well as a kettle, which must have held wash water. And he'd donned the spare shirt she'd seen in his saddlebags. The effect of these changes in the lamplight stunned her—he was one handsome man.

Her face must have given away her thoughts, for he said, "Billy Joe tells me tomorrow is the Lord's Day, so I thought I ought to spruce myself up a little."

"Yes, tomorrow's Sunday, and this is the week I get to take Billy Joe to church, since I don't have to work until suppertime."

Thorn seemed to consider her words, then looked at the plate she was carrying. She saw he was staring at the wedge of peach pie she had placed on it.

"No, I didn't bake the pie," she told him. "This came from Miss Ella's café. Billy Joe tells me he did some dishwashing there for her today, and she paid him with this pie. More than that, she wants him to come back after the noon meal each day and wash dishes for her, and she'll give him fifty cents each time he does it. He's quite proud of himself for getting a job—says he wants to help out with earning money—so I'm proud of him, too."

Thorn grinned. "Reckon you should be proud,

Miss Daisy. That's a responsible thing he did today, getting that job."

She handed over the plate, and sat down on a nearby bale of hay while he sat on his cot. "Thorn, I… I know how Billy Joe got the pie in the first place, and how he came to be washing dishes at the café."

"You do?"

She nodded. "As soon as I came home, Billy Joe confessed to stealing it on a dare from his friends."

Thorn let out a sigh of relief. "I'm glad he told you the truth."

"So am I," Daisy agreed. "Can I ask—would you have told me if he hadn't?"

"No, Miss Daisy, I don't believe I would've."

"May I ask why not?"

"Well, ma'am, boys do a powerful lot of foolish things—things they'd never want their mothers to know about. But at the end of the day, what really matters is whether they're willing to take responsibility for what they've done. Billy Joe did that when he went to Miss Ella and told her he'd taken the pie. Half the reason he was worried about going back to talk to her was that he was afraid Miss Ella would tell you what he'd done, and that you'd feel ashamed. I wouldn't want to put that burden on you, or on him. Not when everything had already been set to rights by your boy."

"Not just him," Daisy replied. "You helped set it to rights, too. He says you insisted that he take it back and accept whatever punishment Miss Ella wanted to dish out." She smiled. "It's a good thing for him that Ella Bohannan is such a kind person."

"I think you can be rightly pleased with your son, Daisy," Thorn said, his face serious. "It can't have been easy, taking that pie back and admitting what he did."

She let him see her gratitude as she met his gaze. "I think I have *you* to thank for making him do the right thing. If you hadn't been here, he would have hid it in his room and eaten the whole thing without telling me, or he'd be defying me about taking it back. He's needed a good man to model himself after, Thorn. Thank you for being that man today."

"I'm not so sure I deserve that label, but I was happy to help," he murmured, as if it hadn't been that big a deal.

Abruptly, Daisy worried that what she'd said would make Thorn get the idea she was hoping he'd stay around and continue to help her keep her son on the right path. She knew that wasn't possible. Thorn Dawson wouldn't be staying. She always had to remember his presence was temporary. But how ironic—a bank robber teaching her son right and wrong.

"I wish…" he began, then his voice trailed off and he looked away.

"You wish what?" she asked, though she knew she should leave it alone and say good-night. *Was he wishing things were different, and he could court her like an honest, free man, or was that only her wishful thinking?*

"Never mind," he said, still not looking at her. "It was just foolishness."

Perhaps it was, and she wasn't about to be foolish, too. "I'm keeping you from eating," she said, rising. "And I better go make sure Billy Joe is washing behind his ears. Good night, Thorn."

"Good night, Daisy. Sleep well."

The words seemed to resonate between them in the dusty, hay-scented barn. *Sleep well.* She thought it might be a long time before she fell asleep tonight.

Chapter Seven

In his dream, he stood at the altar with Daisy, embracing her, giving her his first kiss as her husband. Her lips were soft and impossibly sweet, and he was thinking himself the most blessed man in the world to have won this woman.

Then, suddenly, she was looming over him in the dark stall, no longer just a figure in his dream. She shook him, her glowing lantern jabbing painful shards of light into his sleep-blurred vision. "Thorn! Thorn! You've got to wake up!"

"Daisy? What the…" Whatever her reason for being here and waking him at this late hour, he knew that it had nothing to do with any fantasy he'd formed in his dreams. If she was waking him in the middle of the night, it wasn't to declare her love, but rather because something was wrong. Drawing on the training he'd received as a Texas Ranger, he forced himself to alertness, to sit up and try to focus on the woman crouched over him.

She wore a shawl thrown over her dress, and her hair fell down her back in a night braid, gleaming dully gold in the lantern light.

"It's Billy Joe! He's missing! He's not in his bed!" she cried frantically.

Now Thorn was fully alert. "He's gone? Where could he have gone?"

What a foolish thing to say. If Daisy knew, she wouldn't be out here asking him, near hysterical with fear.

"I was hoping he'd come out here to talk to you," she said, "though I didn't know why he'd do that at this hour..." Tears streaked down her cheeks now, glimmering in the lantern light.

"Was he upset about anything when you went to bed? Did you have to correct him about something?" Was it possible the boy was still vexed about having to take the pie back? Thorn had thought that incident had ended well, but he could have misjudged Billy Joe's reaction...

"No, no..." Impatiently, Daisy shoved her braid back over her shoulder. "Everything seemed fine... but then I woke up feeling like something was wrong, and I went to look in on him, and he wasn't there! Thorn, you've got to help me find him! What could have happened for him just to disappear?"

"What time is it, anyway?" he asked, out of curiosity, not because it mattered.

"I—I didn't look at the grandfather clock as I left the house," she admitted, "but it's got to be after midnight, at least. *Where could he have gone in the middle of the night?*"

"Calm down, Daisy, we'll find him. He can't have gone far," Thorn said, striving to be calm so she could regain her composure. "We'll walk down the street we're sure to find him somewhere."

"But you shouldn't be out walking. Your wounds... And what if you see someone who recognizes you from the bank robbery?" she fretted.

"Daisy, I can't let you go out there looking alone," he told her, and added firmly, "I'll be fine. And I doubt any of the decent people who might have seen me in the bank that day will be out and about at this hour. Maybe Billy Joe and his friends are having a midnight poker game at the saloon," he suggested, trying to inject a little levity into the situation.

But Daisy was past levity. "George Detwiler wouldn't let boys into his saloon," she snapped. "Especially not late at night. But you might be right, Billy Joe might have gotten up to some tomfoolery with those boys he runs around with. Maybe he thought he had something to prove after you made him take the pie back."

Thorn thought she might well have put her finger on it. And suddenly he remembered one of the tales he'd told Billy Joe of his boyhood, how he and his cousins had gone skinny-dipping by moonlight with a jug of moonshine...

It was a possibility that Billy Joe might have followed his example, but Thorn didn't want to suggest that yet. Chances were they'd find him before they got that far. He knew the body of water that gave the town of Simpson Creek its name lay at the end of Main Street, just beyond the little church. Maybe they'd meet the boy before they got that far, Billy Joe strolling toward home, carefree after too many glugs of a shared jug of homebrew, with no idea his absence had been noted.

Moments later, they were walking down the street toward the far side of town, with Daisy glancing nervously around her. "I wish we didn't have to walk right down Main Street," she whispered. "If anyone sees us..."

"There's no one to see us," he told her. "Look, even the saloon's dark as a pile of black cats."

Thorn understood her fear, for a respectable woman wouldn't be out at this hour strolling with a stranger. But she needn't have worried. It wasn't likely they'd encounter anyone, let alone someone she knew. The town of Simpson Creek was well and truly asleep. But to be safe, he'd make sure they crossed to the opposite side of the street when they got to the jail, just in case Sheriff Bishop or a deputy was guarding someone there, and happened to be awake.

There was no Billy Joe loitering outside the closed saloon, nor did they see him as they passed the hotel, the mercantile, the bank, the post office, the barbershop, the jail or the undertaker's establishment. The town was silent but for the gentle sighing of a breeze out of the south and the hoot of an owl from one of the trees in the churchyard as they neared it.

The farther they went, the tenser Daisy grew. "What am I going to do if we don't find him, Thorn?" she asked as they approached the church. "We could go back down Travis Street," she said, indicating a lane that ran parallel to Main. "That'd be another place to look, and it's the street the sheriff lives on. If we can't find Billy Joe, then we'll have to go there to report him missing…" There was an edge of panic in her voice as it trailed off.

Thorn heartily prayed that wouldn't be necessary, and not just for her or the boy's sake. No matter where Billy Joe was, he could imagine the no-nonsense sheriff's reaction to seeing Thorn Dawson was out strolling the street with Daisy, helping her look for her son.

"If I have to tell the sheriff I can't find my boy—"

And then Thorn heard something—so faint it might have been another night bird's call. But he held up a hand and uttered a sharp "Shhh."

There it was again—a distant whoop and a splash.

"Thorn, what is it?"

"I think we've found them," he muttered, already planning to give Billy Joe a piece of his mind, and began striding forward while Daisy still stood there, trying to figure out what he'd heard. But when the next boyish guffaw reached their ears, she ran to catch up with him.

"Wait! They mustn't see you!" she whispered urgently, catching his wrist.

She was right. If the boys saw a stranger with Billy Joe's mother, the word would spread like a prairie fire, and Daisy would have bigger problems on her hands than disciplining a rebellious boy. So Thorn crouched in the undergrowth below a cottonwood, where he could see what was happening, and waited. He'd stay silent and out of sight for now, but he was going to give Billy Joe a talking-to when they got back to the barn, that was certain.

There were perhaps six or more youths frolicking in the creek, which at this location and time of year was shallow enough for boys their age to stand up in. The low-growing plants and saplings that lined the bank were festooned with their clothes.

"Billy Joe Henderson, you come out of there this instant!" Daisy cried, leaning over the water and beckoning, rigid with mixed fury and relief.

Along the creek, boys yelped in alarm and stared in horror at her, some crouching lower in the water, some darting longing glances at the scattered heaps of clothes on the shore, too far away to grab.

Billy Joe stood in the middle of the stream, staring at her. "Aww, Ma, we were just swimmin'…"

"In the middle of the night? You could have drowned! Another boy did, years ago, pulling just such a stunt as this. Not another word out of you," she warned, when Billy Joe seemed about to protest further. "Unless you're going to apologize for running off in the middle of the night and leaving me worried sick about you. Don't even try to justify disappearing like you did without a word to me! Come out of there this minute!" She jabbed her finger at the bank.

Thorn couldn't help feeling sorry for the boy's embarrassment at being found like this by his mother, but privately believed it might do Billy Joe some good. Perhaps in future he'd hesitate before going along with a half-witted plan like this one, knowing how humiliating it could be if he got caught by his mother in the act. Thorn saw the shame-faced look the lad was wearing as he trudged out of the creek and onto the bank, water streaming off him in rivulets that spattered on the bank, and figured that lesson was taking hold. To her credit, Daisy kept her eyes averted and searched through the heaps of clothing. When she recognized her son's shirt and pants, she tossed them to him, then turned her back while he put them on.

"The rest of you better do the same and go home,

or I'll tell your parents," she told the other boys, who remained in the water.

Thorn thought it best to retreat to the churchyard until Daisy and Billy Joe returned from the creek, in case any of the other boys obeyed her command too quickly.

A few moments later, Billy Joe, trudging at his mother's side, started as Thorn emerged from the shadows of the church porch.

"Thorn, you're...*here*?" he quavered, barely looking up, his shoulders hunched.

"Yes, I'm here—or did you think your mother should have to walk through town alone in the dark, worried sick about what had happened to you?"

Billy Joe actually flinched under the lash of Thorn's voice. "I'm sorry, Ma..."

"You're *sorry?*" she repeated, her voice thick with tears. "I was so proud of you for doing the right thing about that pie, and then you scare me like *this*," she murmured, the tears escaping now, gleaming on her cheeks in the moonlight. "Why—"

"I had to show them I wasn't yellow, Ma— like they said I was after I returned the pie," he explained. "So I dared them to sneak out and go skinny-dipping with me..."

Thorn's gaze met Daisy's defeated eyes and he smothered a sigh. For all his protestations of maturity, Billy Joe was still very much a child inside—

one who longed for the approval and acceptance he had never received from his father. How could Thorn leave them, when the boy needed his guidance as much as Daisy needed a man to love and protect her?

Yet he had no choice. The knowledge weighed down his steps as he followed mother and son back to the Henderson home.

He'd thought after their midnight adventure the night before, Daisy would choose to sleep late rather than go to church as she'd originally planned. But she and the boy left, dressed in their Sunday best, just as the bells started to peal from the other end of town. On second thought, maybe she'd figured Billy Joe needed a dose of the Lord more than ever, after his reckless adventures. Whatever her reasons for going, Thorn was glad that they'd departed, since it gave him the chance to do something he'd been wanting to accomplish for what felt like a very long time.

The sun beat down upon his back, but Thorn ignored the heat and took a deep satisfaction from the neat rows of shakes he pounded over the larger of the two holes in the roof of the barn. He'd waited a little while after the steeple bell stopped chiming, so that anyone walking to church wouldn't spot him on top of the barn, and now he enjoyed the fresh air and bird's-eye view of the peaceful, quiet town as he worked. He'd have to listen for the bells to toll again, signaling the end of the church service, to make sure he got inside in time. But if he worked steadily he figured he could get the second, smaller hole closed before he left his high perch and returned to his hiding place in the barn.

He winced as a trickle of sweat found its way to his still-healing shoulder wound, but other than that, he wasn't experiencing any worse pain from his exertion. If he was able to repair a roof, he was as close to being recovered from his wounds as he needed to be. He had no more excuse not to leave and find his way back to the Griggs gang.

The thought sent yet another pang of regret zinging through his soul over what might have been. He would miss his daily encounters with Daisy and their discussions, not to mention her delicious cooking. He'd even be sorry to lose Billy Joe's endless questions and misplaced admiration. Thorn wished he could stay longer and make sure the boy was thoroughly over his admiration of outlaws, but could only hope and pray he might be able to return to Daisy and her son once the job was done. Or if that wasn't possible, that some other worthy man would come along and make them as happy as they so richly deserved to be.

"Get down from there! What do you think you're doing?"

The sudden low-pitched but fiercely whispered question startled him so much he nearly slid off the roof. How had he missed the church bells signaling the end of the service? Looking down, he saw Daisy and Billy Joe staring up at him from where they stood next to the barn. She looked mad enough to spit nails, and he saw her darting anxious glances at her neighbors' houses on either side of hers.

He raised one of the cedar shakes left over from his repair so she could see it. "I've just been fixing your roof, Miss Daisy," he told her calmly.

If he was expecting her to cease her agitation and thank him, he was to be disappointed. *"Get down from there this minute!"* she hissed, her face a study in outrage. "What if someone sees you? What were you thinking, to climb up there in broad daylight where anyone could spot you? And what about your wounds?"

Thorn clambered along the roof to where the ladder was propped against the building, and descended. When he reached the ground and stood by her, he shrugged. "Everyone was in church, near as I could tell—I waited awhile after the steeple bell rang in case there were any latecomers. I figured I'd get down when I heard it ring again, 'cause church would be over. I must've missed the bell and lost track of time."

"They don't ring it at the end of service, just at the beginning," she said, clearly exasperated. "Come on, you've got to get inside." She nodded toward the barn door, then pointed to the house at her right. "What if Mrs. Donahue sees you?"

There was no argument to be made, of course, so he meekly headed into the barn.

"I've got a roast in the oven," he heard Daisy say. "One of us will bring some out to you when it's ready. Billy Joe, go change out of your good clothes before you get them dirty." She swept away before Thorn could say anything—or try to apologize. But perhaps there was no point in apologizing anyway. If he really had been spotted by anyone, then the damage was already done and no apologies he could make would change that.

It was late evening before Thorn saw her again, when she returned from work and brought him supper.

"Hope you don't mind leftovers from the noon meal," she said, proffering a plate filled with a roast beef sandwich on freshly baked bread, along with potato salad and black-eyed peas.

"Of course not," he replied. "It looks wonderful." *Almost as wonderful as she looked to him after his long afternoon spent spinning tales to Billy Joe.* After what had happened last night, he'd made it a point to concentrate on making sure Billy Joe knew about the grimmer side of outlaw life—such as the time Griggs had gunned down one of his men when he'd caught him sleeping when he should have been standing watch.

"I have an apology to make," Daisy said, as soon as they had settled themselves, he on his cot, she on a stool Billy Joe had brought out from the tack room. "I completely forgot my manners earlier when we came home from church and found you on the roof." She nodded upward. "The first words out of my mouth should have been *thank you for repairing my barn roof*, and I failed to do that. I'm sorry, Thorn." Her lovely, deep-set eyes were full of anguish as she faced him.

"There's no apology needed," he told her. "You had every right to be upset. I wouldn't want to do anything to expose you to gossip. No one said anything about seeing me, did they, when you went to work?"

"Not so far," she said. "If rumors come up later, then I'll deal with them. Regardless, I appreciate what you did. It will be nice not to have rain leaking in anymore—not that the chickens ever complained," she added with a faint smile, as one of her hens wandered into the stall, pecking in the hay in search of food. "I hope you're not in too much pain from your exertion?" she asked.

"I am a mite sore, but nothing to really complain about," he assured her. "I'm pretty close to being good as new."

He saw realization of what that meant dawn in her eyes before she spoke the words. "So you'll be leaving before long," she said. "Going back to…those outlaws."

"Yes. I'm sure you won't miss the extra work I've caused you—or the worry that someone will find out I'm here. Don't worry, I won't leave without saying goodbye—to you and Billy Joe."

Did he expect her to say she'd miss him? That she wished he wouldn't go? What a fool he was!

"Billy Joe will miss you," she said. "He really looks up to you. He copies the way you talk, even the way you walk."

Thorn's throat tightened. He didn't know what to say to that. A boy ought to have someone better to look up to than a supposed outlaw. "I'll miss him, too," he finally said. "He's a good boy, you know. He just needs to find his place in the world…"

"I know… I hope I can help him do that," she said wistfully.

Thorn needed to make her believe she could be enough for the boy if he couldn't be there, too. "You *will*, Daisy. You're a good mother," he assured her. "You let him know you care about him, that he's important to you. Not like my father…"

He hadn't meant to say those last words, but it was as if they had been ripped from the deepest part of his heart.

"Not like your father? What do you mean, Thorn?" she asked, her expression puzzled, her eyes searching the depths of his.

Perhaps it was time to get it out in the open. No wound could heal if it was left to fester, ignored and untreated. Only by exposing an injury to light and air was it possible to truly understand what was wrong, and try to fix it.

"As I said, my parents wanted a son—especially my father. Someone to take over the ranch when he was gone, you understand. But after bearing five children already—five that survived, that is, since my sisters told me that there were one or two more children before me who were born too small, too sick or too soon—my mother was getting on in years when she started carrying me. And then, from what I've heard, my birth was...difficult.

"In the end, having me cost my mother her health," he told her. "She was never well afterward and died before I was old enough to remember her. She'd wanted to name me Thornton, after her father, but after she was gone, my father just called me Thorn. He made sure I knew it was because I was a thorn in his side."

"Ohh, Thorn!" Daisy cried, and she threw her arms around him as she began to cry.

He was so astonished—and moved, because no one that he could recall had ever found him worthy of weeping over—that he could only wrap his arms around her and pull her close.

"There, there…why are you crying? Don't cry, Daisy…" he murmured, as he stroked his hands through her hair.

"But that's so awful! How could your father do that to a little boy…to his own son?" she asked, her voice broken with sorrow as she leaned into Thorn's embrace.

"Reckon he knew it was partly his fault that he'd lost my mother, because he kept pushing to get that son. I don't suppose he realized it would cost him his wife—and once that happened, he didn't find it to be a fair trade. My sisters told me that he used to be different—never a soft man, but at least a little kinder. But after that…some part of his heart died when he lost my mother…and he didn't have anything left to give me. Or maybe he wanted me to grow up tough."

Thorn stopped there, not wanting to make any more excuses for the man. He'd long since let go of his anger at his father—choosing to forgive, just as the Lord would want. But forgiveness wasn't the same as understanding, and in his heart of hearts, he'd never fully understand how any parent could reject a child. All Thorn could do was accept that that anger was his father's burden to bear, not his.

And after a painful childhood of never feeling

good enough, he'd found himself in this place, with this beautiful, giving woman treating him as if he was precious to her. Maybe he didn't deserve her affection any more than he'd deserved his father's disdain…but he was glad to have it all the same.

Chapter Eight

Raising her head from Thorn's chest, Daisy murmured, "I'm so sorry that happened to you. I saw what having a harsh father did to Billy Joe, how he's tried to prove how tough he is ever since, and I've done everything I can to make up for it."

"I can see you've done that for the boy," he told her. "He'll grow up all right, is my belief."

"But I want your life to be better, too, Thorn," she stated. "You're a good man and deserve such a good life. Better than you've gotten so far."

"It's been better already," he told her, "just for knowing you, Daisy…" He bent, looking as if he intended to kiss her forehead, but she raised her face and instinctively touched her lips to his.

It seemed to take a long time before their mouths parted, and when they did, Daisy felt as if she couldn't get breath to put her question into words. But she had to know the answer.

"I don't understand why you have to go back, Thorn. On the day you first came here, you told me you weren't really an outlaw. If that was the truth, why must you return to them?"

She saw him blink, and then a weary acceptance shed a faint light into his eyes. "Because it's a job I agreed to do, Daisy. I'm a Texas Ranger."

"But there aren't—" she began.

"—Texas Rangers anymore, since the war. I know. It's the Texas State Police—for now, anyway… But I agreed to infiltrate the outlaws, in order to see them brought down. If I'm successful, there's a big sum of money coming to me as a reward. I plan to get out of the police and use that money to start my ranch. I was looking forward to that, before…before I came here and met you. But now I want that new life almost more than my next breath." His eyes gazed deeply into hers, and she saw that he was telling the truth.

And it gave her reason to fear—for his safety, as she realized the possible consequences for him, if this plan didn't go well.

"But if you're not successful—if the outlaws find out who you are, why you're with them—you could be killed, Thorn."

The statement echoed between her heart and his.

"It's the chance I have to take to be able to start a

new life," he told her. "Don't worry about me, Daisy. Just pray."

She saw that there was no arguing with a choice he had already made, for he was an honorable man, and an honorable man kept his promises. From what he'd said about them, she knew that Texas would be safer once the Griggs gang was eliminated. It was a job that had to be done—but oh, how she wished it could be done by anyone else.

"Come back to us, Thorn...once you get done what you must," she pleaded. "Come back to us."

"I was planning to, Daisy. If I'm able, I promise I'll come back. Wait for me."

"I will," she said. "*We* will."

"Now ain't this a pretty scene," commented an unfamiliar male voice from outside the stall.

Daisy whirled, immediately drawing herself away from Thorn, as he grabbed hold of his Colt and aimed it at the two strangers who stood there, their shadowy faces just visible in the lantern light. She darted a glance at Thorn. He looked furious with himself that he had let his guard down enough that these men had gotten the drop on him.

"Yeah, mighty pretty," muttered the other man. "Good to see you've been keeping yourself entertained, Dawson. No need for that pistol—we're not here to do any harm. Th' boss just sent us to see how you was convalescin', so to speak. And to see if you was well enough to come ridin' with us again."

Daisy edged closer to Thorn and shrank against his side, careful to leave his right arm free. But despite all her instincts telling her to cower, she couldn't stay silent and let these men take Thorn away. "Leave him alone!" she cried, fists clenched. Her heart was frozen with fear, but her words came out strongly—much more strongly than she'd expected. Her husband had trained her so thoroughly to respond to danger, and especially to dangerous men, with cringing fear. Was this Thorn's influence? Did her certainty of his protection give her the courage to be strong herself? "He was wounded, almost died! He isn't well enough to come with you yet—he'll have to rejoin you later."

Even as she said it, she realized they wouldn't believe her, and that Thorn wouldn't confirm her assertion. He was too worried about her safety—just as she was worried about his.

"Go to the house, Daisy," he muttered. "Lock the door. You two polecats stay right where you are."

She read the message in Thorn's eyes: *take down the rifle from where it hangs on the wall and hold tight to it*.

Thorn nodded toward the barn door. He wanted her to get to the house, to be safe. She didn't want to leave him, not knowing what these men might do, but she had her son to think of. *What if Billy Joe woke and found her missing, and came to the barn looking for her?*

"We ain't gonna bother yore lil' nurse," the uglier of the two outlaws said with a sneer. "Shore is nice you could land in such a soft place when you was wounded, with such a sweet lady and all. And she wants to make life better for you—ain't that nice? We heard the whole thing from the tack room where we was hidin'."

They must have sneaked inside once it had gotten dark, before she'd come home from the restaurant. Her mind spun with horror at the thought of them crouching in there, hearing the tender words she and Thorn had uttered. Had they heard Thorn confess that he was a Texas Ranger? No, surely not. If they knew that part, they'd either confront him about it right away or pretend they hadn't heard anything at all, so they could lull him into complacency. If they were willing to reveal that they'd heard some of the conversation, then they must not have heard clearly the part about the role he was playing with the outlaws. For that, she could only be grateful to God.

What could she do? Could she pretend to do as Thorn said, but instead run down the street and fetch Sheriff Bishop? Could the lawman return here in time to save Thorn from going with them? Or would there be a gun battle, with the risk of Thorn being killed in the crossfire? How tragic if her attempted rescue of him resulted in his death.

As if he was reading her mind, she saw Thorn give a tiny, almost imperceptible shake of his head.

Don't try anything. Just go to the house, as I said. Be safe.

It took all Daisy's courage to walk by those two rattlesnakes who stood leering at her, close enough to reach out and touch her as she passed. But it was what Thorn wanted, so she did it.

Once outside, she fairly ran to the house and locked the door behind her. Then she did her best to smother her tears with a dish towel so that Billy Joe wouldn't hear.

"Griggs got a report you was climbin' around on the barn roof like a monkey, Dawson, so he figured you might be recovered enough," Zeke said, once the barn door shut behind Daisy.

"I am," Thorn replied. "I was planning on riding out in the morning to try to find the gang. But since he was kind enough to send an escort, I'll ride back with you tonight—it'll save me having to look for y'all."

He wondered who had seen him and reported back to the outlaws. *Did Griggs have a spy in Simpson Creek?*

Though Thorn tossed off the words as if he didn't have a care in the world, his heart ached that he would not be able to say goodbye to Billy Joe. He'd promised to do so only a few minutes ago as he'd been talking to Daisy, unaware of the threat lurking in the tack room. Would he ever be able to return to the boy and his mother, or would Thorn be one more male who didn't keep his promises to Billy Joe?

The outlaws watched in silence as he fetched Ace's saddle and bridle from the tack room and began to ready his horse. The gelding uttered a sleepy snort of protest at this nocturnal call to duty. All too soon Thorn was mounted and riding northeast out of Simpson Creek, flanked by Zeke Tomlinson and Bob Pritchard, two of Griggs's most ruthless henchmen. Neither would have hesitated to gun him down, he knew, if he'd shown any reluctance to return with them.

They rode about six miles beyond Simpson Creek to the point where the San Saba River joined the mightier Colorado. Here a smoldering campfire with an irregular assortment of seated figures and bedrolls identified Griggs's camp. Thorn had to wonder if they'd been here ever since the bank robbery. Probably not, since the sheriff had made mention of sending out a posse to look for them.

One of the seated figures stood and made his way toward them as Thorn and the other two men dismounted.

"Glad the fellows were able to locate you, Dawson. Good to see you back."

Despite the fact that he used positive words like *glad* and *good*, not a flicker of emotion showed in Gordon Griggs's gaze. His eyes reminded Thorn of those of a shark he'd seen a drawing of one once in a book—flat, black, cold and ruthless. The eyes of a merciless predator.

"You shoulda seen where he was holed up, boss," Zeke chortled. "In a barn, but safe and sound and bein' waited on hand and foot by a purdy widow woman an' a kid, three square meals a day, doctorin'…"

Cold fingers of fear danced down Thorn's spine. How did Zeke know all this? Sure, he'd seen Daisy, but how did he know about Billy Joe? Or the doctoring? Again Thorn wondered who had seen him "climbing on the barn roof like a monkey."

"Ain't that nice…" Griggs muttered, but no warmth reached those suspicious, cold eyes. "How's it happen a doctor tended to you, but not the sheriff? I hear the doc in this town is mighty respectable. Why didn't he turn you in to the law? How come you weren't being cared for inside a jail cell?"

Apprehension did a lively two-step down Thorn's backbone. A wrong answer now and he could end up dead at Griggs's feet. By an effort of will, he kept his gaze away from the pistol always riding at Griggs's hip.

"Respectable ain't the same as incorruptible," he drawled. "I had some money to bribe the sawbones to keep quiet."

"And the widow woman? Did you bribe her, too? Otherwise, what was in it for her? Why would she want an outlaw around her kid?"

Thorn forced himself to utter a suggestive chuckle despite the nausea that churned his stomach. "Let's just say the widow and I reached a certain…understanding," he said, and winked. "Amazing how a few kisses and sweet words will affect a lonely woman."

Guffaws and hoots from the outlaws scattered around the campfire greeted his announcement, but inwardly, Thorn apologized to the lovely image in his mind. *I'm sorry, Daisy, you know I don't mean it.*

Griggs snickered. "Good to know you have such romantic talent, Dawson. Maybe it'll come in handy for the gang some other time." There was an answering chorus of guffaws and grins around the campfire, but Griggs cut it short with a raised hand. "All right, now that you're back, it's gettin' late and we could all use some shut-eye. Gotta be fresh for tomorrow—we're hittin' the Lampasas bank."

Griggs seemed to expect some response from him, so Thorn said, "That's great, boss. Happy to get right back in the game."

Griggs simply nodded in acknowledgment before assigning some of the men to be on watch for the night, as he always did.

While others spread out their bedrolls and pulled off their boots, Thorn unsaddled Ace and made sure he was securely hobbled before finding a place to sleep. His heart had sunk at the news of the upcoming robbery, for there would be no opportunity to tip off the law. Would he ever get enough advance notice of a planned heist that he could set up a trap and bring an end to the Griggs gang's thieving ways? Why hadn't he seen this weakness in the State Police's plan? Was he doomed to attend an endless series of robberies, letting decent people get robbed and sometimes injured, and all the while taking the same risk of getting shot as the real outlaws, because he was indistinguishable from them? Would he be killed before he could ever collect the reward and return to Daisy and her son?

But maybe Thorn wasn't using all the weapons in his arsenal. He hadn't tried praying about it. He'd already asked Daisy to pray for him, and surely she was already storming the gates of Heaven with her prayers on his behalf. As the snores of slumbering men rose around him, he sent up his own silent petition. *Lord, I have no right to ask anything of You, but please protect me and help me succeed in bringing the Griggs gang to justice.*

Daisy smothered a yawn as she turned the chicken parts frying on the restaurant stove, so that they would brown evenly. After watching from her darkened room as Thorn Dawson rode away with the outlaws who'd come to fetch him, she hadn't been able to sleep at all. Instead, she'd lain awake and prayed over and over again—for his safety, and that she would find the right words to tell Billy Joe why his hero had left without saying goodbye.

She'd gone into her son's room when she heard him stirring that morning, for she hadn't wanted him to go out and find the stall empty before she could tell him what had happened. She stressed the fact that the outlaws had not been willing to wait for Thorn to make his farewells—that Thorn had not wanted or planned to leave them so abruptly.

It made her heart ache to see how manfully Billy Joe had struggled to blink back his tears. "He promised to come back to us as soon as he can," she'd told him, but her son had just shrugged as if it didn't matter.

"Who cares?" he'd said. "We got along without him before—I reckon we'll get along without him now just fine. I'm here to protect you, Ma."

Remembering it now, in the restaurant kitchen, Daisy felt a tear streaking down her cheek before she realized it was there. She reached up with the edge of her work apron to catch it.

"Best pay attention to what you're doing, Daisy," Tilly said, reaching past her with a long fork to turn a chicken leg that was getting overdone on one side. "We wouldn't want to burn the mayor's dinner, would we?"

Daisy straightened, blinked and forced a chuckle. She hadn't even seen Tilly entering the kitchen. "No, we certainly wouldn't. It's hot in here," she added, hoping the woman would think the tear was a bead of perspiration.

"So what else is new?" inquired Tilly, patting her own dewy forehead. She winked. "Besides the patched roof on your barn, and the fella doing the patching Sunday morning, that is." She smirked at Daisy's startled expression. "That's right, your handsome workman was *seen,* Daisy Henderson," Tilly announced, a look of triumph on her face. "Mrs. Donahue overslept and didn't make it to church, but when she came in here for a late breakfast, she was quick to tell me she'd been awakened by the sound of someone poundin' on your barn roof next door. She also said he was mighty good-looking, from what she could see from her upstairs window. So who is he, Daisy, dear? Do you suppose he might have some time to come down to the boardinghouse and do some odd jobs for Mrs. Meyers? Or does he solely work for *you*?"

There was a wealth of wicked innuendo in the other woman's tone and a gleam of mischief in her eyes that revealed she was only too glad to have this juicy bit of scandalous gossip to hold over Daisy's head.

She took a deep breath and forced herself to be calm. "Don't be ridiculous, Tilly. He was a traveling man looking for work. I'd saved some money to have the barn roof fixed and he offered to do it in return for a few dollars, a couple of meals and permission to sleep in my barn until he was ready to head back on his way. And I'm sure he'd have been happy to work for Mrs. Meyers at the boardinghouse, too, but unfortunately, he left for Austin this morning. Too bad," she said, feigning regret. "I was very satisfied with the job he did."

But Tilly was not to be so easily vanquished. "And would this traveling workman be the same fellow you were out strolling with the other night? Saw you with my own eyes, I did. But you both looked so *serious*—what was that about?"

Daisy froze at the thought of how much trouble Tilly could now make for her. It was true that there could be no secrets in a town the size of Simpson Creek. She'd been foolish to believe she could have Thorn stay with her and not have anyone notice.

"And what were *you* doing out on the street at that hour, Tilly? As I recall, it was about midnight when I discovered Billy Joe was missing and Th—" she swallowed, realizing she'd almost said "Thorn" "—the workman heard me calling for him in the yard and offered to help me look for him. We found him swimming with his pals in the creek."

"Boys will be boys, I guess." Tilly giggled. "As for me, I couldn't sleep, so I went out for a stroll. That boardinghouse can be so stuffy on summer nights," she added with another elaborate wink. "But you know what a stickler our boss is for propriety in his employees. It wouldn't do to have Mr. Prendergast catch wind of your midnight promenades with the handsome hired man, would it?"

"Tilly—" Daisy began to remonstrate with her coworker, only to freeze in horror at the sight of the very man she had just named standing in the doorway, his arms folded over his cavernous chest and an expression of indignation on his face. *When had he entered the kitchen? What had he heard?*

"Mr. Prendergast? Is there a problem?" she said, pretending to concentrate on the chicken parts she was turning once again.

The proprietor harrumphed. "Only if you consider slow service a problem," he pronounced in his pompous way. "I came through the dining room and found the mayor and his lady waiting on their dinners, and while they didn't complain, it sounds to me as if they'd been waiting for a considerable while. And then I find the two of you back here gossiping— and I believe I heard *my* name mentioned, did I not, Miss Pridemore?" he said, addressing Tilly.

As Daisy feared, the waitress had no scruples about throwing a coworker under the wagon wheels rather than herself.

"Yes, Mr. Prendergast," Tilly said, the picture of innocent virtue. "I was merely reminding Daisy that you insist on the highest standard of morality in everyone you employ—for your female staff in particular—and I pointed out that going out for a midnight walk with a traveling hired man was not, shall we say, *consistent* with that image, especially considering she is a widow with an impressionable son."

The proprietor glared at Daisy and wrinkled his nose as if he suddenly smelled a skunk, while Daisy fought down the urge to call Tilly out as the conniving schemer she was.

"Indeed it is not," he said. "Miss Pridemore, will you be so kind as to serve the mayor and his wife their meals, then come back and take over the cooking while I speak further with Mrs. Henderson about this matter?"

"I'd be ever so happy to do that, Mr. Prendergast," Tilly simpered, with much fluttering of her lashes. "You know my goal is always to serve the hotel in whatever way I can." After plating the food, she flounced out of the kitchen after a last malice-filled, triumphant sneer at Daisy.

With leaden feet, Daisy followed the hotel proprietor out of the kitchen and up the stairs to his office. This was it. Tilly's scheming had succeeded at last. Daisy was about to be fired, and with Tilly and Mrs. Donahue blackening her name all over town, very soon no one would even let her do their laundry. She would be unable to earn any wages, and Billy Joe might well think his mother had earned her disgrace and the precarious situation it would put their family in.

If only she hadn't had to lie to Tilly about Thorn. She'd never been a liar before, but now she was stuck with the story that he was a traveling workman. Though perhaps in this situation, sticking with the false story would be wiser than telling the truth. She couldn't very well tell Mr. Prendergast she'd been harboring a fugitive. That would hardly be—what was Tilly's phrase?—consistent with the high standards of morality for the hotel's employees. Daisy didn't feel she'd done anything wrong, or compromised her morals by taking care of Thorn, and she couldn't be sorry she'd helped save his life. But her own life would have certainly been easier if he hadn't picked her barn to collapse in.

Mr. Prendergast's office was airless and stank of the cigars he favored. By the end of the grueling half hour she spent being interrogated—there was no other word for it—her clothing stuck to her damply, and she felt weak and defenseless as a newborn kitten. But through it all, she had stuck to the same explanation she had given Tilly, and at the end of it, she still had her job.

"But mind your step," Mr. Prendergast warned her when at last he told her she could resume her duties. "If there is any repetition of scandal connected with your name, Mrs. Henderson, you will be seeking employment elsewhere—at the saloon, perhaps."

It was all Daisy could do to smother her indignation. He hadn't even questioned why Tilly had been a witness to her late-night walk down Simpson Creek's main street with Thorn. He seemed to think his waitress could do no wrong.

But at least Daisy had the pleasure of seeing the nonplussed look on Tilly's face when she told the other woman she could resume to her waitressing duties, since Daisy was going back to work in the kitchen.

By this time, however, the noon rush was over and the dining room all but empty. "You might as well take your break," Tilly told her stiffly, when Daisy began to put her apron back on. "If I could handle both your job and mine at our busiest time, I can certainly do it now."

The events of the last half hour had left Daisy without an appetite, but while she'd been pinned to the chair in Mr. Prendergast's office, she'd thought of an errand she'd better do.

Sheriff Bishop needed to know that Thorn had gone back to the Griggs gang last night. Notifying him was the right thing to do, whether or not Thorn's assertion that he wasn't really an outlaw had been true. And while her short break didn't give her time to walk down to the jail—nor did she want to create any speculation about why she'd be visiting such a place, especially when her reputation was already at risk—the back of the hotel was on Travis Street, just a few yards away from the Bishops' house. Prissy, the sheriff's wife, could notify her husband for Daisy, for the sheriff always kept his wife informed of what was going on in town.

Prissy Bishop was one of the kindest women who'd ever breathed, and a fellow Spinsters' Club member, though Daisy rarely had time to take part in any of the social club's events. It had been far too long since she'd had a visit with a friend, and this afternoon she felt very much in need of one.

Chapter Nine

Prissy, with a bright-eyed baby on her hip and a small, yipping dog of mixed heritage dancing at her feet, welcomed her into her home. "Daisy, come in! It's been too long! Houston, don't jump on our visitor! Your timing is perfect, Daisy—I just took some blackberry muffins out of the oven. Can you sit down and sample them, and a glass of lemonade, with me?"

"I can't stay long, but a muffin and a cool drink would be very nice. I see little Samantha is teething," she remarked, having caught sight of a single gleaming white nub of a front tooth as the baby seized on a biscuit Prissy handed her and started gumming it with enthusiasm.

"Yes, and she's been remarkably cheerful about it, as long as I keep her supplied with something to chew on," Prissy said with a laugh. She poured lemonade from a tall jug and handed Daisy a glass. The muffins were already cooling on the kitchen table. The enticing smell of them made Daisy decide she hadn't lost her appetite, after all.

"You said you didn't have long—are you on a break from the hotel kitchen?" Prissy asked, as both women settled into chairs.

Daisy nodded. "I really should speak to the sheriff, but time is short and I was hoping you could give him a message for me."

"Of course."

"I imagine your husband has told you about the fact that one of the bank robbers has been recuperating from his wounds in my barn," Daisy began, then stopped. What if Sam Bishop hadn't confided in his wife as he usually did? What would Prissy think of her then? "Only, he's not really an outlaw—I don't know if Sam told you that…"

Oh, why had she come and opened her mouth? What if she'd lost Prissy's good opinion of her for nothing? What a mess this was turning into!

"Yes, Sam told me about the man—his name is Thorn Dawson, I believe? Goodness, Daisy, how shocked you must have been to find a wounded man in your barn after that awful robbery," her friend said. "Sam told me he's really a Texas Ranger secretly working with the State Police to bring down the Griggs gang. How daring of him! I'm sure Billy Joe is over the moon getting to talk to such a fellow. Sam says he seems a decent sort of man…"

"Yes, he is, but I need to inform the sheriff that a couple of men from the gang showed up last night, and Th—Mr. Dawson—had no choice but to ride off with them. So he's back with the Griggs gang. And if they're gathering up their members, then they might be planning another raid or robbery. I thought Sheriff Bishop would want to know."

Prissy's blue eyes widened. "Oh, dear, and after he fixed your barn roof and everything…"

Now it was Daisy's turn to be startled. "How did you know about that, Prissy?"

Her friend's expression was rueful. "I'm afraid Mrs. Donahue's tongue has been wagging all over town, Daisy, after she saw him up there Sunday morning. And anyone *she* hadn't told, Tilly has. I'm sorry… I've been trying to assure those who brought up the topic that there was more to it than what it appeared, though I could say no more for the sake of Mr. Dawson's safety. But you and I both know that you've done nothing wrong by helping the man recover…"

Daisy gave in to the urge to cover her face with her hands. She could imagine no one would listen to what Prissy had tried to say, after the titillating news they'd heard from Tilly and Mrs. Donahue. Daisy's reputation was in ruins. Despite what Mr. Prendergast had said today, he'd never let her keep her job once he knew how widespread the scandal was. And there was nothing she could do to combat it. The only thing that would quiet the scandal would be if Thorn came forward himself to say that he had honorable intentions toward her, and that he meant to marry her. And he wouldn't do that. Even if she could ask it of him, he was gone now—back with the Griggs gang. There was no safe way to get a message to him, and certainly no safe way for him to respond.

Thorn's safety, while he played this double role, depended on the Griggs gang believing he was as much a criminal as they were. If she tried to tell people in town the truth—that Thorn was planning to return to her, but had to finish his mission for the State Police first—there was too much of a risk that word might get back to Griggs and his men. If the gang somehow heard that their wounded cohort might not be a genuine outlaw at all, and they began to mistrust him, his life could be at risk. Could gossip put Thorn in danger much more serious than any harm it could do to her?

She felt Prissy's gentle touch on her hand. "Don't worry, Daisy. As soon as some new tale gets passed around, everyone will forget about this one. And remember, no Spinsters' Club member is going to stand still while anyone speaks ill of one of their own! Did you know, we asked her once to join the club and she couldn't have been more scornful about it—guess that was a warning what she was made of then! It was as if the idea of women helping and supporting each other to find husbands had never occurred to her, since the only person she ever cared about was herself."

The reminder that she had a strong group of friends who understood and supported her—and who knew what was truly behind Tilly's malice—warmed Daisy's heart, but she didn't like thinking Thorn was out there somewhere in danger, riding with desperadoes.

"You've come to care about this man, haven't you?" Prissy murmured. There was no condemnation in her voice, only sympathy.

Was she that obvious? "What you must think of me, caring about a man who may or may not be an outlaw, falling for him after only a few days," Daisy murmured, trying to hold back tears. Did she look like a desperate widow, needing a man in her life, even though her marriage had been nothing but a misery?

"He must be a very good man, to make you care in so short a time," her friend said. "And remember, there was a time when Sam's reputation was in doubt, too," she reminded her.

Daisy could barely recall the dishonor that had once clouded Sam Bishop's name, when he was exposed as a down-on-his luck gambler who'd stolen a valuable ring from a powerful criminal who'd tried to kill him. By this point she, like all of Simpson Creek, believed in Sam Bishop's integrity as much as they believed the sun would rise each morning.

He'd overcome his past and earned the respect of everyone. Surely Thorn could do the same, especially considering he was only masquerading as an outlaw so that he could see the true outlaws locked away.

"I'll give Sam your message," Prissy promised. "You're right, he'd want to know. And I'll remember Thorn Dawson in my prayers. Keep your head up, Daisy. No one who really knows you will believe Tilly's nonsense. The Lord will work this tangle out, I just know it."

A good friend was like a tonic, Daisy decided—one she wouldn't deny herself in future. Oh, how she hoped Prissy was right!

"I'm right pleased at the way things went today," Gordon Griggs declared as they sat around the campfire that night at a new site they'd chosen to use as a hideout. "None of us wounded, didn't have to wing any townsfolk to keep 'em docile and the idea to rob the Lampasas saloon at the same time as the bank, so we could have ourselves a safe, private celebration complete with whiskey—pure genius, Pritchard!"

"Thank ya, boss," the outlaw said with a grin. "I reckon the only thing we're lackin' now is saloon girls. Next time we'll have to steal us a couple of them, too."

A chorus of guffaws met his sally. The trouble was, Thorn thought, Pritchard wasn't actually joking, and next time, a couple of unlucky saloon girls in the wrong place at the wrong time might find themselves kidnapped and abused. He had to find a way to stop this gang, as soon as possible.

"How 'bout you, Dawson? You enjoy bein' back in the saddle again?"

Thorn kept his features relaxed, knowing that the others were still wary around him after his time away from them. And even before then, he'd been the newest recruit to the gang and therefore viewed with an unending amount of suspicion. He'd felt them watching him during the holdup at the bank and knew it might be a long while before they relaxed around him and trusted him. Infiltrating the group to begin with hadn't been easy; the Griggs gang hadn't stayed on the loose as long as they had by being gullible fools.

When he'd first agreed to this scheme of pretending to be an outlaw, it hadn't mattered to Thorn how long he would have to be with them in order to gain their trust. He wasn't doing anything of lasting value with his life, after all, just trying to avoid being a dirt-poor rancher. And he'd wanted to do something to strike a blow against the gangs that ran rampant in Texas. Nothing he could do would bring Selena back, of course, but fighting against gangs like the one that killed her seemed to be the least he could do to honor her memory.

But now that he'd met Daisy and Billy Joe, and had glimpsed the possibility of an infinitely more satisfying life, each day Thorn had to postpone starting that life loomed ahead of him with agonizing slowness. Plus there was always the possibility something could go wrong and he'd miss out on having that chance with Daisy entirely.

He wondered what she and her son were doing back in Simpson Creek. How was Billy Joe dealing with Thorn's abrupt disappearance without a proper good-bye? Had Daisy been able to explain why he hadn't said goodbye, in such a way that Billy Joe didn't hate him? How was Daisy holding up?

"I had a fine time," he drawled at last, "and like the boss, I always appreciate getting away without the lead flyin'—'specially in my direction, after last time."

There were knowing grins and chuckles around the fire as men passed whiskey bottles from hand to hand. Their haul from the saloon wasn't going to last long at this rate.

"Not me," countered Zeke. "I kinda like lettin' daylight into fancy fools in frock coats, seein' the stupid surprise in their eyes that they've actually gotten shot and might be about to die—and cheatin' death myself."

Thorn had known the other outlaw had a bloodthirsty turn of mind, but the callousness of his words was chilling nonetheless. If he continued thinking that way, Zeke would probably end his days on a gallows someday soon—or bleeding out on the street beside a bank.

Thorn thought about saying something about not being able to count on staying bullet-free forever, but decided to hold his peace. Tomlinson had to know that already, deep down, and if he didn't, he wasn't likely to listen to any advice on the subject.

"Say, boss, mind if I ask you something I was curious about?" Thorn inquired.

"What's that?" Griggs looked at him out of slitted eyes, and Thorn wondered if he'd made a big mistake by speaking up and drawing the suspicious man's attention onto him.

"Just wondering how the fellas managed to locate me at the widow's house without callin' attention to themselves. I mean, Simpson Creek's not all that big a town, but did they search every barn or what? Pretty slick work, however they managed it."

Griggs's grin was smug. "It was, wasn't it? Well, Thorn, my boy, it pays to have informants here and there, and it so happens I have a lady friend in Simpson Creek who'd been keepin' her eyes open, so to speak."

Thorn felt a prickling at the back of his neck.

"That so?" he said, injecting as much of the slavish admiration Griggs seemed to require into his tone as he could stomach. "Boss, you're a wonder."

"Yup. Happens I visited the town a while back, an' while I was havin' a meal at that restaurant in the hotel, I met a gal named Tilly, the waitress there. She was right hospitable, if you know what I mean, and we had ourselves a fine time after she got off work. I didn't figure I'd be seein' her again after the bank heist, but then you went missin', and we was worried about ya…"

Worried I'd get arrested and turn informant in return for a lesser sentence, you mean. Thorn remembered Daisy telling him about the waitress who coveted her job, and felt chilled to the bone at the knowledge that the same woman had a connection with the outlaw leader. From what Billy Joe and Daisy had told him, Tilly wouldn't have hesitated to blacken Daisy's name because Thorn had stayed with her, he was sure, even though she herself was consorting with the outlaws' leader. So now, because Daisy had helped him, she would pay the price in the loss of her good name.

"So…I snuck into Simpson Creek the night after the robbery and went by her place. Asked her to keep an eye out for a fella of your description, and told her where she could leave me a message. Well, sure 'nough, she knew somebody who was out and about Sunday mornin' and happened to see you climbin' around on top of a barn. As soon as my little waitress heard the news, she got in touch with me just like I told her to. We wasn't sure that meant you was stayin' there, but it just so happens you was…"

"So here I am. That was right smart work, boss."

"Women come in handy sometimes, don't they? And the only reward I had to give her was a pair of gold earbobs I took off one of the lady customers in the bank when we robbed it."

Thorn hoped the spiteful waitress would be foolish enough to wear the earbobs around town and have the owner recognize them. Daisy was probably already suffering the consequences of Tilly's vicious tongue, and bemoaning the day she'd met him. She'd never want to see Thorn again. But somehow, if he managed to live through all this, he had to make sure she was all right.

"So what's next for the Griggs gang, boss? Are we gonna lay low for a while?" He should probably have quit with the questions while he was ahead, but in for a penny, in for a pound, as the saying went. Maybe Griggs had drunk enough that his tongue would be looser than it usually was, and Thorn would finally be able to prepare a trap for the gang and its leader.

The others fell quiet as they waited to hear how their leader would respond to the question.

"Haven't thought about it much yet, Dawson. Why? You got a suggestion?"

Griggs's eyes had narrowed again, and Thorn knew his question had been a mite too presumptuous. He shrugged. "Just wonderin' if you thought we ought to get out of the Hill Country for a while, now that we've hit Simpson Creek *and* Lampasas…if you thought it might be getting too hot for us, that's all."

He hadn't meant for that to sound like a criticism, but the implication that the situation might be becoming too dangerous, that Griggs wasn't smart enough or capable enough to avoid capture if they stayed in the area, turned out to be exactly the right spur to the man's excessively large ego.

"Now listen here, Dawson—we didn't get to be the most feared outlaw gang in Texas by actin' yellow," Griggs snarled, showing stained, irregular teeth. "*I* say when a place is gettin' too hot for us, understand? Most of these hick towns ain't even got a telegraph to pass the news of what we done, let alone a sheriff smart enough to catch us. We ain't goin' nowhere unless I say so. An' when I want your advice, I'll ask for it, is that clear?"

Thorn hunched his shoulders and raised both hands palm up to signify submission. "Sorry, boss, I wasn't tryin' to suggest anyone was lily-livered. Just after hearing your story about the waitress, I thought it might be nice for me to take the lady who was caring for me some token of my esteem…if we were still gonna be in the area, that is. If we're movin' on, no problem…" And if he knew where the next robbery would be, he could use the visit to Daisy to tip off Sheriff Bishop while he was there, and not have to convince a lawman in some new town who didn't know him.

Griggs sniggered. "Hopin' to get some time for sparkin' with the lady now that you're on the mend, was you? Must be feelin' yore oats… Well, ya can't go wrong with jewelry, if you get a chance to snatch some—women do like their baubles, don't they?"

Thorn allowed himself to relax a little now that Griggs seemed to have been placated by his reaction.

"Like I said, Dawson, let me think on it a mite." He belched, then let out an enormous yawn. "Shoulda said sleep on it. Reckon I'll turn in…"

"Here's the chicken and dumplings Mrs. Detwiler ordered," Daisy said, pointing to the steaming dish she'd just set out as Tilly entered the kitchen.

Tilly's mouth twisted in an unbecoming pout. "She told me when it was ready to have *you* bring it out."

With an effort of will, Daisy kept a grin from blossoming on her lips. It had to be a blow to Tilly's ego that her campaign to discredit her had met with such a spectacular failure. While a few folks seemed to study her with increased interest, no one had shunned Daisy, treated her like a scandalous woman or even mentioned that they'd heard that a wounded outlaw had been staying in her barn. Everyone seemed to believe the story that her roof was repaired by a working man simply passing through town.

"Oh, Mrs. Detwiler and I are old friends," she said, picking up the hot dish with a towel and heading for the dining room. "She even gave me one of her rose bushes once." Tilly didn't have to know that the older woman, famous for her roses, had done it as a gesture of sympathy when Daisy's husband had been killed.

"Mrs. Detwiler, so good to see you," she said to the woman, who beamed back at her from her seat in the center of the room. "Here's your blue plate special, but we're out of blue plates," she added, as she laid the dish at her place.

It was an old joke between them. The hotel had never had anything but gray-rimmed white china.

"I decided I needed to get out of my house for a while. Tired of my own cooking. How are you, my dear?" asked Mrs. Detwiler. The elderly woman was the acknowledged social arbiter of the town by virtue of her long residence and the fact that her late husband had been a preacher. Yet for all her status, she always had time to inquire kindly after Daisy. "Are you holding up all right?"

Her question, Daisy knew, was a discreet way of asking how she was weathering Tilly's gossip.

"Just fine, thank you, ma'am," Daisy said, giving her a wink to show she understood the deeper context of Mrs. Detwiler's inquiry. "Simpson Creek folks are the nicest folks in Texas."

"*Most* of them," the older woman agreed, with a nod toward the kitchen to indicate she was exempting the waitress. "As my ma used to say, 'What you don't see with your eyes, don't witness with your mouth.' *Some* people haven't learned that yet. How's that boy of yours? I hear he's working at Ella's café. I had breakfast there the other day, and Ella speaks very highly of him."

Daisy smiled. "Billy Joe's doing just fine. He seems to enjoy the job." She started to say she'd better get back to the kitchen, but heard a flurry near the doorway and looked up to see Mr. Prendergast ushering none other than the mayor into the dining room.

"Mayor Gilmore, such an honor to have you dine with us today," he was saying, as he showed him to the most central table.

The mayor thanked him in his affable way as he sat down.

"Get back to the kitchen and I'll bring his order right in," commanded Tilly. But just as Daisy was about to do so, the mayor caught sight of her and beckoned her toward him.

"If it isn't the best cook in the Hill Country," he proclaimed. "Come here, Mrs. Henderson, and tell me what the special is today."

Daisy heard Tilly's barely suppressed sniff of outrage beside her. "Miss Tilly can take your order, Mr. Gilmore," she suggested, knowing she'd pay later, somehow, for any favoritism shown by the mayor.

"I know she can, but I'd like to visit with you for a moment, if that's all right," he said. "My daughter was just telling me what a nice visit you two had the other day."

"It's always pleasant talking to Prissy," she said.

"She makes me feel good. Little Samantha is growing like a weed, too, isn't she?"

The mayor chuckled and slapped his leg. "That's a fact."

"I hope your wife is well?" Daisy inquired. The mayor, who'd been a widower, had recently wed an old friend from his school days, and it was unusual to see him out and about without his Maria.

"She's in Houston, settling the sale of her former home there and visiting old friends, and our cook is taking some well-earned time off, which is why I'm eating at the hotel today," Mayor Gilmore told her.

"Oh, you must miss Mrs. Gilmore tremendously," gushed Tilly, who still hovered behind Daisy. "When will she return?"

"She's coming back on the stage exactly two weeks from today," the mayor said.

"Two weeks from today?" Tilly echoed. "I'll bet you can hardly wait, Mr. Gilmore."

"Indeed I can't," the mayor agreed. "The house seems empty without her. All right, Miss Daisy, tell me about the special today."

It was a gracious dismissal of Tilly, and the waitress knew it. She withdrew, but kept an eagle eye on Daisy and the mayor from the front of the restaurant until Daisy took his order and excused herself to return to the kitchen.

To Daisy's surprise, Tilly took no opportunity to

attempt to pick on her further, even after the mayor departed, but seemed preoccupied with her thoughts. *She's plotting something,* Daisy thought, *but what?*

Chapter Ten

"Still have a hankerin' to visit yore lady friend in Simpson Creek?" Griggs inquired of Thorn the next evening, after they'd spent the day profitably holding up the stage that traveled between Lampasas and San Saba. "I thought after dark I might go see my little waitress, and it occurred to me you might like to go, too."

"Sure, why not?" Thorn drawled, careful to keep his tone noncommittal, as if he didn't care too much one way or the other. Griggs might think he was fooling Thorn, but he wasn't. If they were both in town at once, the outlaw might go nowhere near the traitorous Tilly, but might situate himself so he was in a perfect position to see if Thorn visited Daisy...or if, instead, he used the time to report to the sheriff.

And if that was Griggs's plan, it must mean he suspected Thorn, at least a little. Or was he just being paranoid? Perhaps Griggs really did want to see the waitress.

"Are we meeting to ride back here at any certain time? You weren't planning on staying till morning, were you?" Thorn asked.

Griggs gave a snort. "Have you gone loco, Dawson? Stick around till the town's stirrin' and the law is up and about? Ain't no woman worth that risk, and if you can't accomplish your aims with your lil' sweetheart in a few hours..." He snickered suggestively. "Besides, we're gonna take a couple of the men to stand watch, just in case the law's out prowlin' around... I thought we'd head back about midnight. You still got that pocket watch of yore father's? I can use the one I took off that stage passenger today."

Thorn kept his lip from wrinkling in disgust by an effort of will. The stage passenger, a wizened old man, had wept when relieved of the gold heirloom watch, moaning that it had been his father's. Even if Griggs had no pity, didn't he realize that keeping the timepiece, with those distinctive initials inscribed on the back, "SRT," might be enough to convict him someday?

"All right, we'll meet up at midnight in front of the church to ride back. Sounds like a fine plan. We'll leave after supper, and that should put us in Simpson Creek right about when that one-horse town shuts down for the night, except for the saloon."

Then Thorn thought of something else. Had Griggs learned from Tilly that Daisy worked at the restaurant, too—that their "sweethearts" knew each other and interacted every day? He wished he knew. If Griggs did know, should he ask the outlaw leader not to mention his visiting Daisy, out of concern for her reputation? But he didn't want to bring it up if Griggs didn't know. The outlaw didn't give two hoots in a hailstorm about a widow's good name, and was the cruel sort who might find it entertaining to have Daisy embarrassed by a public scandal, especially if it benefited Tilly by getting her Daisy's higher-paying job. Maybe it was safest to assume that Griggs and Tilly had been too busy with other things when they were together to discuss anyone else.

Thorn had to wonder how Daisy would receive him. Would she have missed him enough to be glad at the sight of him, or would Tilly have blackened her name with gossip enough that she would view him only as the source of her disgrace, and refuse to speak to him? Either way, though, he had to know how she felt.

Too bad he didn't know anything of Griggs's plans for the next few days; Thorn could have Daisy inform Bishop of them so an ambush could be set up. At least he could tell her of the outlaw leader's liaison with Tilly, so Bishop could put a watch on where the waitress lived.

Then he reconsidered. He couldn't chance putting

Daisy in danger by having her inform on Tilly to the sheriff. It was bad enough that Griggs's men had told their leader where Thorn had been staying. If things backfired and Tilly found out who had squealed on her, Daisy and her son might well suffer the consequences. Even if he and Daisy never had a future, Thorn couldn't endanger her further in any way.

Daisy's house was dark by the time Thorn rode up to it. Griggs, accompanied by Bob Pritchard, had ridden away before he got there, turning right after the bank to ride down the alley between the mercantile and the hotel. From Thorn's exploration of the town before the robbery, he knew the boardinghouse sat just behind the hotel, which probably meant Tilly lived there.

Zeke had been assigned to stay with Thorn. Griggs said he was there to protect him from the chance of being attacked, but Thorn was fairly certain Zeke's true purpose was to watch him to make sure he didn't speak with anyone but Daisy. Either way, he was thankful the man didn't seem to think he needed to stay right by Thorn's side.

"Enjoy yoreself, Dawson," Zeke called from the street, as Thorn rode up to the barn. "I'll be out here watchin' the stars. Give me a whistle if you need any help," he added with a snicker.

Thorn wondered how he was going to alert Daisy that he was there. Even if she wasn't furious with

him, she might not want Billy Joe to know he had
come. He didn't know for certain which bedroom
was hers, so he couldn't even throw pebbles against
her window like some lovesick boy.

But he need not have worried. Daisy was sitting
on the back steps that led into the kitchen, a light
shawl draped around her shoulders, and she rose as
he dismounted in front of the barn. Her hair lay in
a thick, moonlight-kissed plait that curved around
one shoulder.

"I couldn't sleep," she murmured as she drew
near. "A few minutes ago, something told me to go
outside and get some air—now I see why. Thorn,
why are you here? Has the Griggs gang been captured?"

"Let's go into the barn," he said, conscious of
Tomlinson sitting on his horse in the shadows in
front of Daisy's house, just a few yards away. "They
haven't been captured yet," he said softly, when she'd
followed him inside. Thorn wished he could have answered in the affirmative. "One of the outlaws had,
uh, business here, and I rode along. I just had to see
that you were all right, you and Billy Joe." He let
himself drink her in, memorizing her features, especially those deep-set blue eyes. In the silvery moonlight he could see the dark shadows beneath them.

"Oh, Thorn…" She sighed, looking down, and
he sensed she was trying to frame her answer so as
to make things sound better than they were. "Yes,

I'm all right, and so is Billy Joe. He just misses you, that's all."

The words were out before he could call them back. "And you? Do *you* miss me, too, Daisy?"

She met his gaze then, and her heart was in her eyes. "Oh, Thorn—I do. Of course I do. And I worry about you..." And then, without conscious volition, she was in his arms, and he was kissing her, his hands curled into the loose tendrils at her forehead, and nothing had ever felt so good in his entire life.

"Daisy, I love you," he said. "And I'm going to do everything I can to come back to you as soon as I can. I want a life with you, Daisy. I want to be a father to Billy Joe."

"I love you, too, Thorn. And you've already been more of a father to Billy Joe than his real father ever was."

She loved him. He couldn't do more at that moment than contemplate the enormity of her admission. And kiss her again as he thanked God for her, until finally he knew he had to stop kissing her or he'd never be able to let her go.

"I was seen, wasn't I, that morning I was up on your barn roof. That's how the outlaws located me, apparently. Whoever saw me must have told someone, and word spread from there."

She nodded ruefully. "Mrs. Donahue next door overslept that day and missed church. She heard the banging, and when she looked out her window, she saw you. She came into town for breakfast and told Tilly—the waitress, remember?—and Tilly tried to cause a scandal and get me fired." Then, to Thorn's surprise, Daisy chuckled. "But it didn't work. Our boss gave me another chance, and no one else who knew me would pay her any mind. The people of Simpson Creek just have better things to do."

"It's a town I'd be proud to live in," he agreed. He waited a moment, then said, "Should you let Billy Joe know I'm here? It's up to you, of course, but I can stay for a little while."

Daisy stared at him, an agony of indecision painting her features. "I… I don't think so, Thorn. If he wakes up and finds you here, that's one thing…but it was too hard on him, when you suddenly had to go that last time. To see that you're back, but hear that you'll need to leave before morning would be difficult for him to take. Better to wait, I think, until you can stay."

She was probably right. And anyway, with Tomlinson on watch, it was better that Billy Joe not come outside. And as Daisy had said, the boy had had enough experience with significant male figures disappearing from his life.

But Thorn had a while before he was to meet Griggs at the church, so he might as well treasure the time with the woman he had come to love. After settling themselves on a bale of hay, they shared stories of their lives, with Thorn peeking at his pocket watch every so often so the time didn't get away from them.

Daisy told him about Billy Joe's birth, and how happy she had been to have a baby to love, since she'd learned she couldn't depend on his father's affection. She also told him how scared she had been to put an innocent baby in the path of her violent husband. She told him about how her husband had been arrested for kidnapping the teacher, too, and how he had later been killed in a prison riot. Touched by her tragedy, he found himself telling her about his first love, Selena, and how she had been killed in an ambush by the very outlaws he'd been chasing. This had been before, during the war years, when he could still call himself a Texas Ranger. While he was speaking about Selena's loss, he changed his mind about not telling Daisy about the waitress. If she wasn't forearmed about that other woman, it might somehow lead her into an ambush, too.

"Daisy, I want you to be very careful around that Tilly," he whispered. "She's dangerous—"

"Dangerous?" Daisy gave a little laugh. "Thorn, she's only gossipy and spiteful. Don't worry, I can handle her."

He framed her face between his hands. "No, listen to me, sweetheart. I mean it. She's dangerous. She's the one who Griggs is…uh, sparking. He's with her right now. A woman who'd knowingly ally herself with an outlaw…well, there's no telling what she might do. She's already agreed to pass information over to him. She's the one who told the gang that they could find me here. Be very careful how you deal with her—for your safety and Billy Joe's."

Daisy's eyes had gone wide in the dim light. "But shouldn't we tell the sheriff he's here, this Griggs?" She started to rise. "Thorn, we could tell Bishop and he could capture him—this very night! It'd be over. You wouldn't have to go back to them—"

He took hold of her wrists and gently pulled her back down to the bale she'd been sitting on. Then he told her about Tomlinson on watch outside, and she stilled immediately.

"I *should* say you shouldn't have come, especially since you brought an outlaw with you. But since he's one of the ones who already knows where we live, I don't suppose it matters," she said with a shrug. "And I needed to see you," she declared, a fierce spark shining in her eyes. "So I can't be sorry. But Thorn, I could let Bishop know about Tilly later. He could set a watch on her—"

Her voice had been rising from a whisper due to her excitement, and Thorn gently laid a finger over her lips. "I thought about that," he admitted. "But I think it's too risky. She'd sic the gang on you and the boy out of pure spite if she found out. And if she managed to get word to Griggs that she was being watched, he'd suspect that I was the one who'd passed the word along to the sheriff. No, I just want you to keep an eye on her. Watch what she does—but don't go to Bishop unless you have no other choice. Trust me that I will do everything I can to bring these outlaws to justice. And pray," he said, kissing her forehead.

"Oh, I do trust you," she assured him. "And I have been praying. I've learned what 'praying without ceasing' means, as the Scriptures say we're supposed to do."

All too soon, it was nearing midnight and time to go. Leaving her felt like ripping a part of his heart out and leaving it here. But he knew it would be safe in Daisy's keeping.

The next afternoon, Tilly was whistling as she came into the kitchen with the latest order.

"You're in a good mood," Daisy observed, forcing herself to smile. Since she knew who was responsible for the other woman's unwonted cheeriness, she found it almost unbearable.

"Had a visit from my sweet beau last night," Tilly said with a wink. "That always boosts my spirits. I highly recommend it—having a beau, that is." She gave a trilling laugh that stung Daisy's nerves like sandpaper on an open wound. As if now that Tilly had recommended having a beau, Daisy would immediately start seeking one, as though she had never thought of it before.

"Do I know your beau?" she asked, wondering

what Tilly would say. Thorn wouldn't want her to toy with the waitress like this, but she found the other woman's behavior maddening.

Tilly shrugged. "I don't think so," she said. "He lives a ways out of town. But one day he's going to take me away from all this…" she said, waving her hand at the kitchen with its hot stove and racks of pots, pans and dishes. Her eyes danced with a secret glee.

Did Tilly think the outlaw was going to ask her to marry him? Then wed her in the church, in front of the whole town, before carrying her off on a big white horse as if she were a fairy princess? If she did, she was living in a dream world. But maybe she didn't even care if marriage was not a part of the bargain, as long as she had someone to shower her with stolen finery.

"Well, until that day comes, maybe you'd better take this order out to the customer," Daisy said, dishing up a slice of roast beef dripping with gravy and mushrooms.

"Boys, I usually don't talk over plans with y'all very far ahead of time, as you know," Griggs announced that night by the campfire. "But I got wind of…an opportunity, shall we say, that would require some advance work on our part—and an extra helping of guts to carry it out. But I have to know if you're up to it." His dark eyes glittered in the fire-light.

"What is it, boss?" Pritchard asked. "You know we're up for anything you want to do, especially if there's a big prize."

Thorn took a sip of his coffee. Might this be the opportunity he'd been waiting for, a chance to set a trap for Griggs and his gang?

Griggs grinned. "The prize is big, all right, but so's the risk. When I was in town last night, I caught wind of some news. The mayor's wife is outta town visitin' in Houston, and she'll be comin' back by stage exactly two weeks from yesterday."

Now several of the men were leaning forward, their faces avid. "What did you have in mind, boss? Robbing her stagecoach? What if she ain't carryin' no big valuables?" one asked.

Griggs chuckled. "Nothin' so picayune as that. No, this'd be a bigger escapade than we've pulled off in the past, and I gotta know if you're willin' to take on the risk before we go any further."

He waited until every member of the Griggs gang was staring at him. Thorn thought some of them might be holding their breath.

"All right. Mayor Gilmore is the richest man in San Saba County. I propose we stop the stage, kidnap his wife as she's traveling back to Simpson Creek and hold her for ransom. Then, after he pays up, we let her loose and head for the border, where we can live like kings on the ransom money for the rest of our lives. What do you say?"

"What if he won't pay, boss? What then?" asked another of the outlaws, across the fire.

"Oh, he'll pay, all right. She's his second wife, and they ain't been married that long, so it's well known that he's powerful sweet on her—sweet enough to part with whatever we ask to get her back safe. No fool like an old fool, as they say," Griggs added with a guffaw. But then his features hardened. "But we've got to be willing to set consequences and stick to 'em if he tries to play fast and loose with us."

"What does that mean, boss?" asked Tomlinson, who sat near Thorn.

"We've got to tell him we'll kill her if he don't pay up in time—and mean it. Maybe slice off a finger or two to show him we mean business."

There were audible gasps around the campfire. "That ain't no picayune plan, for certain," someone muttered.

Griggs shrugged. "As I said, if the idea's too much for you boys, we can keep robbin' banks an' stages. But this is the chance to pull off a huge heist and get away to where we kin live like kings ever after. No more getting' shot at and dodging posses. I just need to know none of you is gonna go yellow and back out at the last minute."

As always, an appeal to the outlaws' pride got guaranteed results. There was a chorus of "I'm in" and "let's do it" and "I always did want to live 'cross the border with my own dark-eyed senorita."

"You game, Thorn?" Griggs asked, gazing at him out of the corner of a narrowed eyes.

"Sure, why not?" he replied, his tone lazy. But his mind was racing. Did this plan have something to do with Griggs's rendezvous last night? Was Tilly the one who had informed him of Mrs. Gilmore's travel plans? If so, the waitress was more evil than he had imagined. And if she really had played any sort of role in the plan, then she was an accessory who could go to jail right along with her outlaw lover if it could be proved.

All that made her more dangerous to Daisy, if the woman ever found out Daisy's outlaw guest was really a lawman in disguise who wanted to put her beau in jail. For that reason alone Thorn was more determined than ever to bring Griggs and all his allies to justice.

Chapter Eleven

"I was thinkin' about this project of ours—the kidnapping," Griggs said to Thorn the next afternoon. Most of the outlaws were taking a siesta, having eaten a heavy noon meal of stolen barbecued beef. If the law came to arrest them now, Thorn thought, the only trouble they'd have would be in waking some of them up to take them away.

"Something I could do to help in the planning?"

"Yup, as a matter a' fact, there is. Strikes me that while we know when that mayor's wife's coming back, I don't rightly know the route the stage takes, or the schedule. Do you?"

Thorn shook his head. "Can't say as I do."

"Then I'd like you to go find out. Go to the stage stop in Simpson Creek and ask about those things. And it's all right by me if you want to fit in a little visit with yore woman while you're there."

Your woman. While Thorn would never think of Daisy in such a coarse way, the idea that she was his made him want to smile. He'd have to do some hard riding to get to town before the stagecoach manager was gone for the day, yet he could manage it if it meant seeing Daisy. But was his desire to do so getting in the way of clear thinking? Thorn didn't know if it was safe for him to be seen in Simpson Creek. "I'd be right happy to do that, boss. But… what if someone recognizes me, riding around town in broad daylight?"

"Don't fret, I thought of that. Just so happens I got a frock coat and trousers that Zeke took off a stage passenger one time that oughta fit you. It was stupid of him—Zeke's a lot fatter than that passenger was, so no way that poor fellow's duds would've fit him, but we saved the clothes in case one of us needed to go disguised as someone respectable. Iffen you was to shave, you won't look nothin' like that desperate fellow they last saw robbin' their bank."

Thorn had to smile at the thought. A ranger disguised as an outlaw disguised as a respectable man. His situation just kept getting more and more ironic.

Once he'd shaved and put on the frock coat, though, he had to agree that he looked nothing like a bank robber. The clothes might as well have been tailored for him, and they were fancier than anything he'd ever owned. He could probably pass for a traveling doctor or preacher. Daisy might not even recognize him at first sight.

As he gazed at his freshly shaved face in the mirror he'd propped in a tree branch, he thought about what Daisy would be doing when he arrived. She'd still be cooking supper, and no doubt cleaning up, until mid-evening. And Griggs had said nothing about sending any of the outlaws with him.

If Daisy wouldn't recognize him, chances were that Tilly wouldn't, either. Daisy had said that the waitress had only actually seen him just once, when she'd caught a glimpse of him and Daisy walking to the creek the night Billy Joe sneaked out to go skinny-dipping. So Tilly had seen him only from a distance, in the dark. Which meant he could probably get away with having a respectable dinner right at the hotel without anyone suspecting him of being anything different from what he appeared to be—a perfectly respectable man just passing through town.

"You look like a parson," Griggs observed when Thorn presented himself before leaving.

He grinned. "Parson Dawson, that's me. Thanks for lettin' me do this, boss. I'll get your information for you."

"I know you will," Griggs said. "And you're welcome—I like to keep my men happy."

I'll be happiest seeing you behind bars, Thorn thought. *But this'll do until I can.*

* * *

"Did you see that fine-looking fellow at the middle table?" Tilly asked when she came to pick up the latest order at the narrow pass-through window between the kitchen and the dining room.

Daisy peered out without any real interest, but spotting the tall fellow in the black frock coat, snowy-white shirt and string tie, she had to agree there was nothing wrong with the waitress's eyes. He was a handsome man, all right. As handsome as Thorn Dawson would have been, she thought, if he possessed clothes like that and was clean-shaven. She had to laugh inwardly at the thought. Thorn had probably never worn a frock coat in his life.

"Yes. He's certainly not from around here," she murmured, turning back to the ham fritters she was making.

"His name is Reverend Dinwiddy, and he's from Austin," Tilley said, smug in her advanced knowledge. "He's been called to a church north of here to take over as their parson. Funny name for such an attractive fellow, isn't it—Dinwiddy?"

Daisy nodded absently, but went back to her work. *So the man who could have passed as Thorn's brother was a preacher.* She'd have to tell Thorn about it, if she ever saw him again.

The preacher ordered ham fritters and corn, and when Tilly picked it up to take it out to him, Daisy took advantage of the opportunity to peer out at him again.

Reverend Dinwiddy watched Tilly as she approached with the meal, but as the waitress bent over to deposit the plate in front of him and pour his coffee, he raised his eyes to the pass-through window and, seeing Daisy looking at him, winked.

It *was* Thorn Dawson, or she wasn't Daisy Maxwell Henderson. *How dare he come here like this?*

She forced herself not to look again for a long while, lest Tilly notice and also realize who the "parson" really was. *How was it possible that the girl hadn't recognized him already?*

Yet she wasn't looking at the man through the eyes of love, and Daisy was.

When she finally couldn't resist peeking out again though, the "parson" had evidently finished his meal and left. She sighed. *Had Thorn really taken such a risk to come here, for no other reason than in hopes of catching a glimpse of her? Was it possible he loved her that much?*

It would be something to think about as she fell asleep, Daisy thought, as she applied herself to the last stack of dirty dishes that stood between her and going home for the night. Tilly, who would never think of helping her finish, had already left, after boasting about the nice tip the preacher had left her.

Perhaps Daisy would even dream about him. She wished she could have spent some time with Thorn, but for now, this brief glimpse would have to suffice until he could return to her for good. *Lord, please hasten that day.*

Night had fallen by the time she gathered up her paper-wrapped package of supper to take home to Billy Joe. It was so late that Daisy wondered if she'd find him still awake. She hoped Ella had given him something to take home to eat after his shift there.

It was a good thing Simpson Creek was such a safe town to live in—except for the rare bank robbery, she thought, as she lit the lantern and locked the kitchen door behind her. Otherwise she'd have been nervous about walking the dark streets alone, especially going past the saloon.

"Can I walk you home, Miss Daisy?" said a voice from under the shadowy eaves of the back of the hotel, startling her so much she dropped her package and nearly let go of the lantern, as well. "Here, let me get that," Thorn Dawson said, bending over to pick up what she'd dropped.

"What are you doing here?" she demanded in a smothered whisper, looking around her lest Tilly be lurking in the shadows. "Don't you know what a risk you're taking?"

"Don't worry, I made sure Tilly had left before I came back here to wait for you. She's been gone an hour or more, so I think we're safe. But I was in town and I had to see you."

"You did? Why? Oh, *Thorn*," she said, as he swooped down and pulled her into his embrace. As his lips touched hers, she decided *why* he was here could wait a little while to be explained.

He'd left Ace tied up at the hitching rail at the saloon, where he wouldn't be noticed. They picked the horse up and Thorn led him the rest of the way to Daisy's house. When they reached it, there was no need to make a decision as to whether to tell Billy Joe of his presence or not, for the boy was sitting on the back stoop, waiting for his mother.

"There you are at last, Ma. I was getting worried... Thorn!" he cried, and rushed toward him. "What're you doing here?"

Thorn gave him a hug, then told him an abbreviated version of what had brought him to town, concluding with "But I can't stay much longer, I'm sorry to say. Ace and I have to be getting back."

Daisy and the boy's faces fell. "Can't you come in and just stay while I eat what Ma brought me for supper?" Billy Joe asked.

Thorn's eyes met Daisy's to see what she thought. She hadn't invited him inside the house during the whole time when he'd been recuperating in her barn, for fear of scandal, he knew. He saw her peer carefully at her neighbor's house, which was dark, then she squared her shoulders and turned back to Thorn and her son.

"Yes, that would be nice, Thorn. Please come in. We can sit in the kitchen."

The kitchen was small and homey, Thorn saw when he stepped inside, with a round table in the center and a cast-iron stove at one end. Daisy raised the glass and lit the lamp on the table, and Thorn and Billy Joe sat down while she reached into a cupboard for a plate, knife and fork, and set out the food. She placed the pot of coffee she'd brought with her on the stove to reheat.

"Ham fritters, yum! And apple pie, my favorite dessert! But…Mr. Thorn, have you eaten? I'd be happy to share with you…"

Thorn saw Daisy beam at this showing of good manners on her son's part. "Actually, he ate at the restaurant. Didn't you?" she said with a twinkle in her eye, then told the boy how Tilly had mistaken him for a traveling preacher.

"Boy howdy, Mr. Thorn, you're the daringest man ever was," Billy Joe enthused, then went back to attacking his supper with boyish gusto. "That Tilly must be blind as a fence post if she didn't recognize you."

"Billy Joe, some respect for your elders, please," Daisy said, but he could see she was hard-pressed not to smile.

"Yes, ma'am," Billy Joe said, then yawned after swallowing the last bite of pie.

"I'd better be going, Miss Daisy," Thorn said reluctantly, setting his cup down. These few minutes sitting with her and her son had felt so relaxing and natural. It had given him a glimpse of what being part of a family would be like—especially *this* family— and he was loath to let it go.

"Young man, say good-night to Mr. Dawson. It's time you got ready for bed," Daisy said.

Thorn extended a hand to the boy, and Billy Joe shook it manfully.

"You keep on helping your ma, Billy Joe. I'll be back to see you when I can."

"I will, Mr. Thorn, I promise."

Daisy walked Thorn out to the barn, where they'd left Ace in a stall. "You never said what you were doing in town today, but I'm guessing you didn't come just to see me."

He shook his head. "No, though you're certainly worth a special trip, Daisy. As it happens, Griggs sent me to research some details about stagecoach routes," he told her. "Can you let the sheriff know that the gang is finally planning something that I think I can give him advance warning about?"

"Of course, Thorn."

He then laid out the plan as far as it had been developed at this point.

Daisy clapped a hand over her mouth after Thorn finished talking. "Griggs actually thinks they can get away with kidnapping the *mayor's wife* and holding her for ransom?" Her voice rose to a squeak. "Don't they realize how risky that will be, how many things could go wrong? Someone could get hurt!"

"Yes, but all they care about is the reward they're hoping to get with the ransom payment. They're planning to live like kings across the border after that. But don't worry, they're not going to succeed, because we know about it in advance. We're going to use that knowledge to ambush the gang and capture them. And that's how I'll get out of the gang and out of the Rangers, or State Police—or whatever they want to call themselves these days—and live happily-ever-after with you and Billy Joe," he told her with a lopsided grin.

Then he grew sober again. "Be real careful when you speak to the sheriff, Daisy," he warned her. "Make sure no one overhears you, or sees you going to the jail. We think Tilly's the one who supplied Griggs with information about Mrs. Gilmore's travel schedule, though I have to wonder how she came to know of it."

He saw Daisy's eyes narrow at the mention of the waitress.

"I know exactly how it happened. The mayor told her about his wife's plans the other day when he came in to have dinner at the restaurant," she told him. "That poor innocent man was just making conversation—little did he know he was speaking to a Jezebel! But don't worry, Sheriff Bishop's wife and I are friends, so it's not unusual for me to visit their home," she assured him. "Though it makes me furious that another female, someone I *work* with, would stoop so low as to *help* the gang plan to kidnap Mrs. Gilmore, and maybe even hurt her. What can Tilly possibly hope to get out of conspiring with criminals that is worth the risk to good, honest people like the Gilmores?" Daisy's blue eyes flashed sparks of fury.

He shrugged. "Hard to understand, isn't it? But I've seen how Griggs operates. He makes big promises to the men—and probably does the same with Tilly. If she's the sort to want fine things, and not care too much about who she has to hurt to get them, then I could see her falling for his fancy words."

Daisy was thoughtful for a moment. "She likes fine things well enough, but at heart, I think what she truly wants is the same thing I want, a man she can trust." Her eyes were luminous as she faced him. "I almost feel sorry for her, when I think of it that way."

His Daisy had a soft heart, Thorn realized. It was one of the things he loved about her. "All the same, treat her with the same care you would a rattlesnake. She's dangerous."

"I will, I promise. And you be careful, too, Thorn."

And then it was time to kiss Daisy goodbye and ride back to the outlaw camp.

"The man at the stagecoach stop in Simpson Creek said a person coming from Houston would take the train from Hempstead, a little outside of Houston, to Austin, and catch the stage from there," Thorn told Griggs when the outlaw finally left his bedroll the next morning. He'd been asleep when Thorn had arrived in camp the night before. "Based on when they're expecting her back, I'd say that Mrs. Gilmore would arrive in Austin the second day at noon, and leave on Friday at 6:00 a.m. on the Sawyer and Risher stagecoach line. I figure she'll plan her travel so she's not in Austin more than overnight by herself. The stage gets to Lampasas at 4:00 p.m. and leaves the next morning at seven, getting into Simpson Creek at four."

Griggs rubbed his stubbly chin as he considered. "Much as I'd love to add train holdups to our list of accomplishments, I expect snatching the woman from the stage would be easier," he said. "Fewer people traveling, less chance of armed guards. Now we just have to figure out whether to stop the stage afore it gets to Lampasas or when she's on the final stretch to Simpson Creek."

"There's less towns and lawmen between Lampasas and Simpson Creek than from Austin to Lampasas," Thorn pointed out, thinking it would also be easier to involve Sheriff Bishop in the capture of the gang closer to his own town, and quicker for Thorn to return to Daisy afterward, if all went well.

"Good point, Dawson, and good work, getting this information," Griggs said. "No one acted suspicious at the stagecoach stop, did they, when you asked about this?"

"They all took me for a parson, like you said, boss. I told 'em my wife was traveling to join me after a visit to Houston to see her mama, and I wanted to be sure to meet her when she got in."

"All right, we'll wait for the stage somewhere between Lampasas and Simpson Creek. There's plenty of daylight left," Griggs added, after casting a bleary eye upward at the sun. "Why don't you and Tomlinson and Pritchard ride out and scout us a likely place? I want a spot with plenty of cover, close to the road, but not near any houses or ranches where we're apt to be spotted by nosy neighbors."

Thorn gave a mock salute and went to roust the other two from their poker game. He only wished it could all be over sooner.

Chapter Twelve

Leaving the sheriff's office, Daisy hurried back down the street to the hotel, her stomach growling because she'd used her midday break to visit Sheriff Bishop and inform him of the Griggs gang's plot. Hopefully, she could snatch a biscuit or two to tide her over till supper without Tilly seeing her and tattling to Mr. Prendergast about it.

The sheriff had been grim-faced when told that the Griggs gang planned to kidnap the mayor's wife as she traveled home by stagecoach. "I don't like it," Bishop had said, rubbing his forehead as if trying to soothe away a sudden headache. "Too much could go wrong, even with Dawson there to help us and make sure we save the mayor's missus. Instead of sending a force to ambush the gang, I ought to have the mayor send his wife a telegram telling her to stay put till we could have a whole regiment of cavalry escorting her home."

Daisy hadn't foreseen that the sheriff might take such a notion, nor had Thorn, apparently, and now she saw Thorn's chance to get out of the outlaw gang slipping away. If the outlaws stopped the stage and Mrs. Gilmore wasn't inside, they might get away before anyone could capture them.

"Oh please, don't do that," she'd said. "Give Mr. Dawson this opportunity to capture the gang, so he can put them behind bars and end this dangerous masquerade of his. Every day he spends with the outlaws is a chance his real identity could be discovered."

"Don't fret, Miss Daisy, the likelihood of the federals agreeing to cooperate with a Southern lawman would be slim as a grasshopper surviving a red ant hill," the sheriff had muttered, and then his next words startled her. "You've really grown to care for this Dawson fellow, haven't you?"

Once again she'd wondered, was she as transparent as that? The idea had dismayed her. *If the sheriff could see right through her, how many others could?*

But she wouldn't lie. "Yes," she'd admitted, not daring to look him in the eye.

"And does he feel the same way?" Bishop's voice had been neutral, yet she'd sensed a tenseness in him as he waited for her answer.

"I believe so," Daisy had said.

"He ought to, that's for certain," Bishop replied. "You deserve a better hand than what you've been dealt lately, you and the boy. I'd like to see you have what my Prissy and I have."

The care in his words touched her deeply, and caused her to remember that he had been a gambler in his past. *If a gambler could become a respected lawman and beloved husband, perhaps that meant even Daisy Henderson could have an honest man who loved her.* "Thank you, Sheriff. I appreciate that."

"I'll do everything I can to get him back to you safely, Miss Daisy, as much as it lies in my power."

After a long day spent on the road between Lampasas and Simpson Creek inspecting possible holdup sites, Thorn and the other two outlaws reported back to Griggs, recommending a location where the road ran between two outcroppings of rock just after a sharp bend in the road. The driver would be forced to slow his team to make the turn and would not be watching for danger, only to be presented with a line of outlaws, guns trained on him, when he came around the rocks. The place was ideal from the standpoint of having a thick cover of trees, as well as a little creek running nearby to water the horses, yet was far from any ranch or cabin. Better yet, it was an easy distance from a cavern with a hidden entrance that would be the perfect place to hide and guard the kidnapped mayor's wife until the ransom had been brought to an agreed-upon location and left there. After the ransom was paid, Mrs. Gilmore would be escorted close to Simpson Creek and let loose. She would walk back into town, unharmed and grateful to be alive, but unable to describe her captors because she would have been blindfolded during her captivity. They would take care not to use each others' names while they had her in their custody.

"Sounds perfect," commented Griggs, after they'd discussed it over supper.

It was even more ideal for another reason. Thorn had noticed a draw nearby, where the lawmen whom he would have warned of the kidnapping could lie in wait to ambush the ambushers. It was far enough away from where the outlaws would be that any slight noise they made wouldn't be heard by the gang, but it had easy access to the road. Thorn would need one more trip into Simpson Creek to set it up. He'd send a message to the Rangers—State Police, he corrected himself—and notify Bishop so the sheriff could coordinate plans with the other lawmen in the area.

"Yeah, boss. After that," Tomlinson said with a grin, "we can spend the rest of our lives sippin' tequila and cuddling with our pretty senoritas across the border. I kin hardly wait."

They'd all be starting new lives after the kidnapping, Thorn thought, but not the leisurely lives of ease in Mexico they had planned. Instead, the outlaws would be starting years in prison, if not life sentences. Some of the more violent ones had deaths on their records, and might end up facing a hangman's noose. And with God's help, he'd have a new life, too, Thorn thought, with Daisy at his side, and no need to ever again draw a gun on another human being.

Daisy ladled out vegetable soup into two bowls and sliced a loaf of crusty bread for her meal with her son. Though it had been perhaps the tastiest soup she had ever made, there weren't many takers among the restaurant customers. As warm as it had been at midday, and even still at suppertime, no one had wanted hot soup, so Mr. Prendergast had criticized her for making it. Only now that darkness had fallen had the heat of the day begun to abate.

But hot or not, Daisy was hungry. By the time she had finished talking to the sheriff, there had been no time for a dinner break and she had had to dive back into cooking.

"Why don't we thank God for the food first?" she gently chided Billy Joe, seeing that he had already devoured half his soup. She folded her hands together and said a quick grace.

"How was business at Miss Ella's café today?" she asked a few minutes later, hoping to break the silence punctuated only by the sound of a hungry boy slurping soup.

"Okay…"

So much for that conversational gambit, she thought wryly, as Billy Joe turned his attention back to his bowl.

"Did you see your friends after your shift was done?"

He nodded, but didn't meet her gaze.

"What's wrong?" she finally asked.

He glanced at her, then shrugged. "Now they're making fun of me for having a job," he groused. "They said I was more fun when I didn't have to be so *responsible*." He said the word with contempt. "They said my nails were clean as a girl's from all the dish washing." He held his hands out to show her.

"And what do you think of what they said?" she asked carefully, wondering if she would make things worse with her question.

He shrugged again. "I don't care what they say." But his posture said he *did* care, and had been hurt by their words.

"And what do you think Mr. Dawson would say about your being such a dependable worker?" she asked.

"'Ain't none of them earning wages to help their families,'" he said, doing a creditable imitation of Thorn's deep, drawling voice.

She saw him square his shoulders as he spoke, and was encouraged by that. Even if he never returned, Thorn had made a positive impact on her son's behavior.

Billy Joe laid his spoon down. "Ma…" he began, unusually hesitant. "Ma, I miss Mr. Thorn."

"I do, too, Billy Joe," she admitted.

"When's he coming back?"

Now it was her turn to shrug. She dared not tell him anything about the plans the gang had to kidnap the mayor's wife, and Thorn's role in thwarting it. It was safer right now for her son to believe Thorn was really an outlaw. And if he didn't know about the planned kidnapping, then he wouldn't be filled with worry about it—the way she was.

"I don't know, son. Soon, I hope."

"Me, too. I think he'd like to quit outlawin' and marry you."

She had risen to slice a couple pieces of the cake she had brought home for dessert, but now she was so astonished at what Billy Joe had said that she nearly dropped the knife.

"You do?"

Billy Joe nodded with enthusiasm, then wiped his mouth on his sleeve. "I think you should marry him, Ma. He'd be a good pa. And you wouldn't have to be alone when I grow up."

Sometimes Billy Joe said the most astonishing things when she was least expecting them, she thought, feeling the pricking of tears in her eyes. She still wasn't sure how she felt about Thorn. She knew she loved him, and believed him when he'd declared he loved her. But she still didn't know what kind of life they could have together. The future for the two of them would depend on what he did, on how he kept the promises he made.

"Well, you keep him in your prayers, Billy Joe, and if it's God's will, it will happen," she said. *Please, Lord, let that happen.* "Remember, 'trust in the Lord with all thine heart…'"

"I will. I want it to be soon."

Oh! Me, too, son. You can't imagine how much. She wondered how Billy Joe would like finishing his growing-up years on a ranch, working at Thorn's side. He wouldn't have his no-good friends in Simpson Creek to pal around with and to lead him down bad paths. His life would be full of rigorous chores and hard work, but somehow she didn't think he'd mind too much, with Thorn as his stepfather.

"So you don't think the widow will follow you to Mexico?" Griggs asked, when Thorn broached his request to go to Simpson Creek for a last visit with Daisy before the kidnapping. "Sure you're not underestimating your charm, Dawson? You need some lessons in romancing? I'd be glad to give you some tips. My woman can't wait to join me across the Rio Grande, though she knows she'd better continue to please me, or I'll trade her in for a dark-eyed Mexicana."

Thorn tamped down the urge to punch Griggs in the face for even mentioning Daisy in that tone, as well as the temptation to voice exactly what he thought of the treacherous waitress who had made Daisy's work life so miserable and who was willing to risk the life of the mayor's wife just to satisfy her own greed.

"Naw, I don't reckon she'll leave Simpson Creek," he said, carefully keeping his tone neutral, as if it didn't matter all that much. "She's got the boy to think of, and I don't reckon she wants him living with an outlaw... And I don't think she'd much like living in a country where she'd be a foreigner."

"Maybe she'll change her mind when she realizes you're kissin' her goodbye forever, and she'll leave her son behind," Griggs suggested with a snicker. "Don't reckon she'll have another chance for a good-lookin' fella like you to leave his boots under her bed, 'specially with that young cub of hers around."

Thorn set his teeth, knowing his control would eventually slip if the outlaw kept jawing as he was. It was useless telling a man like Griggs that his feelings for Daisy were more honorable than that. "Maybe she will, but I don't think so."

"All right, go make your farewells tomorrow, but be back in time to get some shut-eye. The day after that's our big day, and I need all my men to be 100 percent on their toes."

"Here's the last order," Tilly said. "It's the mayor. I'm going on my break, so I'm sure he'll be glad to have you bring him his meal rather than me. And don't expect me back real soon," she added, as she pushed open the kitchen's back door. I'm going to go eat at Ella's café."

"Why? There's plenty of catfish left," Daisy pointed out.

"Ugh! You know I hate fish," Tilly snapped. She gave an elaborate sniff. "The whole kitchen stinks of it."

"There's still some sliced roast beef from yesterday," Daisy offered. "I could fix you a sandwich."

"Don't bother," Tilly replied. "I need some fresh air, after all this fish smell."

The kitchen *did* smell of fish, but what could they do but use up what Mr. Prendergast had hooked when he'd gone fishing the previous day on the San Saba River? He was so proud of his catch. Fortunately, most of the restaurant's patrons were fond of fried catfish.

Daisy sighed as Tilly exited the back door without another word. Walking down to Ella's café at the other end of town and waiting for her order to be cooked before she could even begin eating, the waitress would be gone much more than her allotted half hour. But Mr. Prendergast never seemed to mind, even though Daisy had to do double duty, waitressing and cooking, while she was gone. At least she would be able to greet Mr. Gilmore without Tilly looking jealously on, she consoled herself.

Perhaps Tilly even had the grace to be ashamed to face the mayor, knowing what the outlaw gang had planned for his wife. Surely even Tilly would have to feel a little ashamed of herself when faced with the woman's husband. But Tilly's conscience was really none of Daisy's concern, so she pushed those thoughts out of her head and set to work frying the mayor's catfish.

"That looks delicious," Mayor Gilmore said a few minutes later, when she brought it out to him.

"I hope you like it," she told him. "Mrs. Gilmore will be home from her trip soon, if I remember rightly?"

"Tomorrow, if all goes well," he replied, beaming. "I'll be a happy man."

It was all Daisy could do to keep smiling, knowing about the planned kidnapping, but not being able to say a word of warning. She felt so guilty. It would have been better if she hadn't known anything about it, she thought. She'd be in an agony of worry till it was all over. But if she hadn't known about it, Thorn couldn't have set up the ambush that would hopefully result in her rescue and Thorn's release from his dangerous lawman-in-disguise role, she reminded herself, and felt a little better.

"I'll pray for a safe journey for her," she murmured. "Enjoy your meal, sir."

The day dragged after that. Now that she'd been reminded that the kidnapping was to be tomorrow, she couldn't help wondering if Thorn would come to see her, and what he was doing today. Were all the plans in place?

Tilly came back after being away for an hour— far longer than she was supposed to be gone, and unapologetic as ever. "I had chicken and dumplings at Ella's café—very tasty! Oh, and I had a nice chat with your son," she announced breezily as she came in through the back door. "You didn't tell me he was working there."

Why would I? It's not as if we ever have a friendly conversation, Daisy thought, even as she wondered what Tilly and her son would find to talk about. Aloud, she said, "I didn't? Yes, he's quite proud of earning a wage." She didn't like the idea of Tilly speaking to her son, and wondered what they could have talked about. Billy Joe knew how Tilly treated his mother, after all, and he tended to be protective of her, sometimes to the point of being rude to those who he believed snubbed her. But Tilly exaggerated a lot; likely the "nice conversation" had been no more than an exchange of hellos.

"I could have sworn I saw that nice Mr. Dinwiddy riding into town as I reached Ella's," Tilly remarked. "You remember him? That traveling parson who came to the dining room the other day?"

Daisy froze. Was Thorn in town, disguised as he'd been when he came to the restaurant?

"Oh? Did you say hello?"

Tilly shrugged. "I waved, but the man rode right

on by as if he didn't know me," she said with a sniff. "Maybe it wasn't him, after all, but he looked like him..."

"Now that you're back, I'm going to take my break," Daisy said. "Don't worry, there's no one new in the dining room so far." *Had* Tilly seen Thorn in his disguise? Was he even now in Simpson Creek?

"Aren't you going to take some of that delicious catfish to eat?" Tilly asked snidely, just as Daisy reached for the doorknob.

She shook her head. "It's all gone. The mayor asked for seconds, he liked it so much. And I already ate while you were gone," she said. "I nibbled that roast beef between orders, since I was so hungry, so I'm just going to take a walk and get some fresh air."

As much fresh air as I can get between the restaurant and the sheriff's office, anyway. Maybe she'd be in luck and find Thorn there, making plans with Bishop about tomorrow.

Chapter Thirteen

It was hard to tell which man was more startled when she threw open the door of the sheriff's office, Thorn or Bishop. Both men jumped to their feet.

The sheriff found his voice first. "Miss Daisy? Is something wrong?"

Thorn just stood there watching her, his eyes asking the same question. She saw that he was dressed as Dinwiddy, the traveling preacher, just as Tilly had said.

"I thought you might be here. Tilly said she saw Mr. Dinwiddy riding into town."

Thorn grimaced at that. "Yes, I saw her. I was hoping if I didn't wave back, that'd convince her she was mistaken about recognizing me. Guess it was too much to hope for that she'd be occupied with work if I came to town during the day."

"She should have been," Daisy agreed grimly.

"But she is now, so she won't know I came here. I had to see you, Thorn…" She felt suddenly awkward, with the sheriff looking on. "I—I was wondering if everything was in place for tomorrow…when Mrs. Gilmore comes back on the stage. The mayor was in the restaurant, and he's so pleased she's coming home."

The men exchanged looks, and then Thorn turned back to her. "Yes, all the arrangements are made. The sheriffs' offices in the area know where we're stopping the stage, and they'll be lying in wait not far from us, ready to capture the Griggs gang. But you shouldn't be here, Daisy—it's too dangerous. I don't think Griggs had anyone follow me to town, but I can't rely on it. Someone might see you…"

"I—I'll go out the back way," she murmured, and headed for the rear door. Before she could push it open, though, Thorn caught her wrist.

Bishop suddenly became absorbed in a pile of wanted posters on his desk.

"Daisy, it'll all be okay," Thorn assured her, looking down into her eyes. "Before you know it, Griggs'll be behind bars and we'll be able to start a life together."

"I'm praying for you," she said, and then she was in his arms, and he was kissing her, and she quite forgot there was anyone else in the room but the two of them.

* * *

"Tilly tells me she had a nice chat with you at the café," Daisy said that evening as she watched her son pick at his food. She'd saved a serving of catfish for him, but perhaps he preferred catching them over eating them, she mused. He seemed distracted, almost as if he was as consumed with thoughts of tomorrow as she was. But he didn't know anything about the planned kidnapping of the mayor's wife.

"Yeah. It was okay," he mumbled, keeping his eyes on his plate.

"Was it? What did you two find to talk about?" Daisy asked, trying to keep her tone one of mild interest.

Billy Joe shrugged elaborately. "Nothing much. You know…how did I like working for Miss Ella and Mr. Bohannon, that sort of thing. She was nice…"

Nice? Tilly was never nice unless there was something in it for her, Daisy thought tartly, and immediately chastised herself for the uncharitable idea. Maybe the woman was trying to reform, and it would be a shame if no one gave her credit.

"Maybe you'll like dessert better than you did the catfish," she stated, bringing out the bowl she'd kept covered until now. "Peach crisp."

"Yum!" Billy Joe said appreciatively. But Daisy thought he still looked preoccupied.

"Yes, well, it's getting late. Finish up and then it's time for bed." She wasn't sure *she* would be able to sleep a wink, but Billy Joe would probably be sawing logs inside five minutes.

"Ma, I love you," Billy Joe said a few moments later, after he had eaten every last crumb. "You're the greatest ma a guy could have."

"I—I love you too, son," she murmured, watching as he walked out of the kitchen, down the hall and into his room. It wasn't unknown for him to say "I love you" to her, but he didn't say it often, and now the timing struck her as odd. Had he sensed something was about to happen tomorrow?

Thorn returned to the outlaw camp before time to turn in, as he'd agreed, only to find that Tomlinson and Pritchard were missing around the suppertime campfire. When he mentioned it to Griggs, however, the outlaw leader was unperturbed.

"Those two had some unfinished business to take care of," the outlaw leader said. "Nothin' t' worry about." Yet there was something in Griggs's eyes that made Thorn worry more, not less. There were four horses missing from the picket line, not just the two that Tomlinson and Pritchard rode. What were they up to?

The two still hadn't returned by the time Thorn stretched out on his bedroll and finally dropped into an uneasy doze, only to be awakened a couple of hours later by the sound of horses approaching camp.

Who was supposed to be on watch? Had Bishop

decided to spring the trap before they could even kidnap the mayor's wife?

It was only Tomlinson and Pritchard returning at last, but they weren't alone. Thorn saw a woman dismounting from one of the horses, and thought for a horrified moment that the two outlaws had decided to take a woman prisoner. But it was clear she was no captive when she uttered an excited squeal and went streaking across the campfire area, dodging bedrolls and men newly roused from sleep to throw herself into the arms of Gordon Griggs.

"There's my sweet woman!" the outlaw leader crowed, wrapping her in an embrace.

"Here I am, all ready to skedaddle over the border to Mexico with you!" she trilled, before planting a big smacking kiss on Griggs's scarred, whiskery cheek, to the hooting cheers of the gang.

Disgusted, but wary of letting the others see his distaste, Thorn shifted his gaze back to the other newcomer, and saw to his horror that it was Billy Joe Henderson.

Thorn crossed the distance between where he'd been standing and where the youth was dismounting before he even had time to think about it. *"What are you doing here?"* he demanded in a harsh whisper.

The face Billy Joe raised to him in the flickering light was dull with misery. "I… Miss Tilly, she said I could come with her and be an outlaw with you. She says you're holdin' up some stagecoach tomorrow.

But I didn't think you'd want me doin' that, 'cause of how it would affect Ma, so I said I wouldn't. Then she said if I didn't come, the gang would sneak into town and kidnap Ma, this very night." His gaze left Thorn's and he peered around the camp as if to check that Daisy wasn't there.

Fury blazed within Thorn. "You shouldn't have done that, Miss Tilly," he said, even as she turned to face him in Griggs's embrace.

"Gordon thought we needed a little *insurance,* didn't you, sugar?" Tilly purred, gazing up at her outlaw lover adoringly.

Thorn was chilled by her open declaration that the gang leader didn't trust him fully.

Griggs's eyes gleamed like silver slits as he looked back at Thorn. "I didn't think it would hurt to be a little more certain you were 100 percent committed to our success, Dawson. Tilly had come to suspect that might not be so…"

The waitress met his gaze without blinking. Somehow she'd seen something, overheard something… Thorn didn't know what, but it seemed his careful disguise had become threadbare, at least to this sly woman, and as a result, Griggs had a hostage who Thorn would do anything to protect.

"I've given you no cause to think I'm two-faced," he insisted. "So you're going to send an untried boy into danger tomorrow when we hold up that stage the mayor's wife'll be on—aren't you afraid he might affect your 'success', too?" Thorn asked.

"Simmer down, Dawson," Griggs ordered. "He ain't gonna be with the men. He's going to stay with Tilly in the cave. He kin help guard our hostage."

One glance at the woman confirmed she wouldn't hesitate to be as ruthless with the boy as Griggs would have been.

"You said I'd get to ride with Thorn!" protested Billy Joe, his hands clenching into fists at his sides as he faced Tilly, then Griggs. "I want to stick with him, not stay behind like some baby!"

If the kid wasn't careful, he'd end up in danger this very night and not have to wait until tomorrow, Thorn thought. "Hush up, Billy Joe," he snapped, praying the boy would have sense enough to heed the warning. "You have to prove yourself before you can be an outlaw," he added, though he suspected that by this point, Billy Joe had no desire to be an outlaw left. After all the stories he'd told the boy about the rough, unpleasant life of an outlaw, this taste of the reality of it all had finally made the point. "And proving yourself means following orders and not talking back."

Billy Joe turned to him. "But what's this about kidnapping the mayor's wife, Mr. Thorn? I didn't know it was gonna be *her* stagecoach! Mrs. Gilmore's a nice lady. They shouldn't be botherin' her—"

"She won't come to any harm, Billy Joe," Thorn

assured him. "They're just going to hold her for ransom." He wished he was as certain as he sounded. There would be nothing to stop the gang members from offering the mayor's wife all sorts of indignities if they were sure of escaping punishment. And if there was any hint that her husband might not be willing to pay the ransom... "Time to get some shut-eye. You can curl up on my bedroll," he said, pointing to where his blankets lay.

"But what will you sleep on, Thorn?" Billy Joe asked.

"I'll lie back against that tree—the one near the bedroll, see? I'll be fine." He wouldn't sleep sitting up, but with the arrival of the boy and the complications that represented, sleep wouldn't come again tonight, anyway. If anything happened to Billy Joe, Daisy would never forgive him. And Thorn would never forgive himself.

Early the next morning, Daisy tiptoed down the hall at dawn to peek in on Billy Joe before she left the house to start cooking breakfast at the hotel. Seeing her sleeping son had always been an encouragement to her, a reminder that however hard her life was as a widow, she was not alone...

But this morning his bed was empty. Had he awakened early and gone out to feed the chickens for her? A prickle of alarm danced up her spine, for he'd never done that before...

And then she saw the scrap of paper on top of his pillow, and dashed across the room to pick it up.

"Ma Im with Thorn. Tillys gunna bring me. Dont worry about me" was scrawled across the paper.

"Oh, dear God!" Daisy shrieked, as soon as the words made sense. She flew out the door, not stopping at the hotel, but running until she reached the jail. How had he gotten a horse to ride to reach Thorn? She very much doubted he'd had the money to rent a horse at the livery.

Outside the jail, two saddled horses stood at the hitching post. Inside, she found Sheriff Bishop standing with Deputy Menendez. Both men held mugs of hot coffee and appeared ready to ride. Of course! They were going to ambush the kidnappers, she reminded herself.

"The outlaws—the Griggs gang—they've got Billy Joe!" she cried, as soon as her lungs allowed her enough breath to get the words out. Her hand was trembling as she held out the note.

The sheriff read it in grim silence, then put a palm on her shoulder. "We'll bring him back to you, Miss Daisy, with God's help," he said, his eyes kind. "Are you working today?"

She gave a shaky nod. "I'm supposed to…"

Bishop said, "Then you go on to work, and try to pray instead of worry."

Not worry? Go to work? How could she do that? Daisy stifled a hysterical laugh as she stared at the sheriff, then turned on her heel and pushed open the door, heading for the hotel. She was going to wring Tilly's neck when the waitress showed up, she vowed, for she knew deep inside that the other woman had had something to do with luring her boy into danger. She'd known there was something her son hadn't told her about his conversation with Tilly at Ella's café, but Daisy certainly hadn't expected anything like this.

There was usually an hour between the time she reached the restaurant to start breakfast preparation and when Tilly arrived, for there was very little for the waitress to do until opening time drew near. Normally Daisy treasured the peace and quiet while she set out place settings for breakfast, which disappeared as soon as Tilly started slamming plates down on the tables and rattling silverware out in the dining room, while humming some tune off-key. Now, however, Daisy left off stirring pancake batter and cracking eggs to walk into the hotel lobby every few minutes, staring out into the street to see if she could see Tilly coming as the time to open the restaurant drew near.

"Something wrong, Mrs. Henderson?" inquired Mr. Ellington, the hotel worker who manned the registration desk during the night, after her fourth trip out.

"Tilly isn't here and it's time to open," she said, pushing back a stray curl that had fallen over her forehead. She wanted to add, *And she's taken my boy with her, the evil woman!* But Daisy didn't want to tell anyone her son might have chosen to run off with the outlaws, and merely added, "I think Mr. Prendergast should be notified."

"Dear me," sighed Mr. Ellington, rolling his eyes as if to see through the ceiling to the second floor room where the proprietor lived. "He won't like waking up to that, will he? Still… I suppose you're right. We'd better let him know." He hefted his bulky body off the chair he'd been sitting on and headed for the stairs.

A late riser who was used to leaving his kitchen staff to cope on their own with breakfast, Mr. Prendergast was *not* pleased to be awakened with the news that Tilly hadn't shown up.

"Mr. Ellington, you'll have to go down to the boardinghouse and see if the silly woman's still abed," he announced, ignoring the fact that the man's overnight shift was already done and it was time for him to go home. "And if you find her, she's to report to me before she starts work. Mrs. Henderson, you'll have to take care of the dining room *and* the cooking until he returns with Tilly," he told Daisy, lowering himself onto the chair Ellington had just vacated.

Daisy nodded. She'd already guessed she'd have to do Tilly's job as well as her own. And it was Sunday, which meant business would be slow till noon, and then it would be overwhelming. *Lord, help me!*

"I hope she's just overslept," she murmured, twisting her apron in her hands. She knew in her heart that Mr. Ellington wouldn't find Tilly, but Daisy couldn't say so without revealing the fact that her son had gone with her to join the outlaws. As it was, when Mr. Prendergast found out what her boy had done, Daisy would lose her job for sure, for he would think too much scandal was attached to her name—even though he was losing his waitress at the same time. With his high standards for conduct, he'd prefer to have no staff at all than to have scandal surrounding even one of his employees. But that seemed of little importance now. *Please, Lord, keep my son safe, despite his foolish choices.*

Chapter Fourteen

"It just figures we'd be stuck waitin' for that stage on the hottest day of the summer," grumbled Tomlinson, after they'd been settled in their hiding place for about an hour. "What time is it due here, anyway?"

"About one," Thorn replied. If all had gone according to the plan he'd made with Bishop, the sheriff's men were already nearby, too, ready to capture the would-be kidnappers, though so far they hadn't betrayed their presence by so much as a horse's whinny.

"Didn't you say they left Lampasas at six in the morning? It ain't *that* far. What takes so long?" Bob Pritchard complained.

"You fellers stop yer bellyachin'," Griggs growled. "You're worse than a thousand buzzin' flies. You're forgettin' how rich we're all gonna be when we get done with this. I think that's worth a little sweat."

Thorn lowered his voice to answer. "They must have stopped at a station halfway between Lampasas and Simpson Creek to change teams and feed the passengers."

"So the team'll be fresh," Tomlinson commented, sounding a little worried, as if he feared they could outrun the outlaws.

"But the driver's stomach will be full, and he'll be wishin' he could take a nap," Pritchard said, then chuckled. "Poor fool won't be suspectin' a thing."

Thorn suppressed a grin. Pritchard must never have taken the stage, if he thought the food at the stations was plentiful enough to make the driver drowsy. By the time the man supervised the changing of the teams, there would be only a few morsels left at the table for him.

Lord, please, let my plan succeed. Let the sheriff and his men capture the outlaws as soon as they have taken the mayor's wife, and let no one be injured in the process, including the stagecoach driver—keep him from offering resistance. Let me receive my reward so that Daisy and I can be wed and go on to a new, better life. Amen.

Thorn started to raise his head, then remembered Billy Joe, who'd been most indignant to be consigned to Tilly's custody. *And, Lord, one more thing—please give Billy Joe the common sense to stay where he is and not give that treacherous woman any trouble, for there will be no true victory if he is harmed.*

* * *

By noon, Daisy thought she was truly going to lose her mind. The surge of customers into the restaurant, dressed in their Sunday best, signaled that the church service was over. She no longer had time to worry about Billy Joe or Thorn or Mrs. Gilmore—there was just a never-ending stream of order-taking and cooking. And yet her worry remained, nagging at her soul, and worsened by Mr. Prendergast, who lurked at the passageway between the hotel and the restaurant, watching with his sharp, beady eyes, yet never offering to help. So far the strain hadn't caused her to get any orders wrong, but it was just a matter of time.

"Daisy, so good to see you," a woman gushed. "But why aren't you in the kitchen? It's your cooking we've come for."

Daisy blinked and took a look at the speaker. It was Sarah Walker, the doctor's wife, and Milly Brookfield, her sister, was sitting right next to her. Their numerous offspring, as well as their husbands, surrounded them.

"Hello, Sarah, and you, too, Milly, and Dr. Walker, and Mr. Brookfield!" Daisy hoped her enthusiastic greeting would hide her agitation. "Yes, it's just a bit busier than usual here today, what with Tilly, our waitress, being off sick, so I'm doing both jobs."

Milly's mouth dropped open. "You're *what*?" She took a look around her, seeing the tables full of diners, with others still at the door waiting to be seated. "Oh, no, that's impossible. No one can do that." She stood. "I'll be your waitress until the rush dies down. Just give me some paper, a pencil and an apron, and I'll take your orders. No arguing, now."

Daisy thought she might get fired just for allowing Milly to help, but the chance to finally catch up on the cooking and stop feeling so in over her head was worth getting in trouble. So she ignored the consternation in Mr. Prendergast's eyes that she could see from the pass-through window between the kitchen and the dining room, when Milly in her borrowed apron started zipping around the tables, taking orders, refilling water glasses and coffee cups, cleaning tables when diners were done and ushering new customers into those places. Free to concentrate on her cooking, Daisy caught up with the orders and people got their food, and finally the crowd began to thin out.

Daisy kept Milly's meal on the stove until business had slowed down enough for her to eat it, and she was just thanking her for her extraordinary help when Mr. Prendergast made his way over to the table.

"Mrs. Brookfield, we're always honored when you're able to come in from your ranch and dine with us, but for helping us today, your family's meal is on the house," he told her in his unctuous way.

"Happy to help, sir," Milly responded. "You won't

mind if your hardworking cook sits down for just a moment with us, will you?"

Daisy guessed he would have liked to say that she should get to work on the pile of dishes that were no doubt awaiting washing in the kitchen, but how could he, with Milly Brookfield, founder of the Spinsters Club and wife of an influential rancher, smiling so winningly up at him?

"Of course not," he purred. "Just let us know if there's anything else we can get for you folks." He retreated to the passageway as if to watch for more diners.

"I can't thank you enough," Daisy said, sitting in a chair Dr. Walker had brought from an empty table. "My feet are plumb worn to a frazzle. I never would have been able to keep up with both jobs if you hadn't helped, Milly."

"Happy to assist, as I said," she repeated. "And happy to have a chance to share a meal with you. How's that boy of yours, Daisy? Last I saw him, he'd grown a foot taller at least."

"Yes, he's been keeping busy working for Ella at her café..." Daisy began, but then her voice trailed off. In the last hour, she'd been so busy frying and basting and boiling and dishing up food, she'd had no time to spare for worrying about Billy Joe. But now the whole situation came back to her in a rush, and suddenly her cheeks were awash with tears. "Oh, Milly, I'm so worried about him..." She covered her face with her hands, horrified that the proprietor might return and catch her sobbing into her apron.

"Let's just go into the kitchen and start on the dishes, shall we?" Milly said, urging her to her feet and steering her gently in that direction.

Once the door of the kitchen swung shut on them, it all came spilling out of Daisy—the whole story of how an outlaw had come to stay with them after he was wounded at the bank robbery. And how Billy Joe had grown to admire the man—who wasn't really an outlaw but a State Police officer, working secretly to infiltrate a gang—so much that he was even now waiting alongside him to halt the stagecoach and kidnap the mayor's wife. And how she and Thorn Dawson had come to fall in love.

Milly, elbow deep in dishwater, took it all in stride, as if she heard such fantastic stories every day. "You poor thing," she murmured. "You've had to be strong for so long, my dear..."

Daisy knew the other woman was referring not only to her son, but to her marriage to the brute who had been Billy Joe's father, and his subsequent death in a prison riot. Yes, she'd had to be strong. She sniffed and added the soup bowl she was drying to a stack on the prep table.

"Thanks for listening. Prissy's the only other one who knows all this about Thorn, because of Sam being the sheriff, of course—although I suspect your sister, Sarah, has known about the wounded outlaw in my barn, too, since her husband was treating him."

Milly smiled. "You couldn't have picked better confidantes," she said. "Daisy, I'm sorry neither I nor the Spinsters Club have been more of a help to you through all the troubles you've been shouldering since long before Thorn Dawson came to town. With me out on the ranch and with the young'uns to keep up with—"

"There's nothing anyone else could have done," she insisted, not wanting Milly to feel guilty for Daisy's own bad choice of a husband.

"Well, it sounds as if once this escapade is done, there'll be a wedding taking place," her friend said as she dried her hands. "When that happens, the Spinsters Club can help you plan the celebration."

Milly's caring, encouraging smile nearly started the waterworks again. "Thanks, I'd like that. But I'm afraid I won't draw an easy breath until Billy Joe— *and* the mayor's wife—are both safe at home again."

"I'll be praying," Milly assured her, "for all of you."

"It's coming! The stage is coming! It's 'bout half a mile around the bend!" Pritchard yelled as he rejoined the gang waiting in their hiding place. Since he'd found a shortcut over a hill that led from their place of concealment from the road, he'd been sent to watch for them.

"Get to your spots, boys—this is it," Griggs called out, gesturing at them. Everyone pulled their bandannas upward from their necks to cover the lower half of their faces.

Griggs's words echoed in Thorn's brain as he reined Ace out into the rutted road as the others were doing. *This was it.* The culmination of all his careful planning. In the next few minutes, he would either have successfully planned an ambush of the ambushers, which would lead to his reward and the start of a new life for him—or the ambush would fail and he'd be viewed by the authorities as one of the kidnappers. For if Bishop's men weren't able to surprise and subdue the gang, and harm came to Mrs. Gilmore, Thorn would likely be held as responsible as the others, even if the State Police confirmed that he'd been sent on their orders to infiltrate the gang. No one but Daisy and Billy Joe would believe he was a lawman in disguise then. He trusted Sam Bishop to be a man of his word, but what if he wasn't?

"Trust in the Lord with all thine heart; and lean not unto thine own understanding..." The verse from Proverbs he'd heard Daisy quote came back to him now. *"In all thy ways acknowledge Him, and He shall direct thy paths."* Thorn had entrusted this plan to God, hadn't he? It wasn't something based only on his understanding, so why wouldn't the Lord bless

it? It wasn't the Lord who brought these doubts into his mind now, at the last minute…

I trust You, Lord. Please protect me, Billy Joe and Mrs. Gilmore, and let all go according to Your plan.

"Whoa!" Griggs called out as the stagecoach rounded the bend. As if by some unspoken signal, he and the rest of the outlaws blocking the road fired their pistols into the air. The terrified team of horses whinnied in panic, reared and pawed the air with their hooves. For a moment Thorn was afraid they would cause the stage to be overturned, with the startled horses stampeding, dragging the coach on its side with its passengers helpless to save themselves.

Amazingly, though, the animals settled once the report of the guns died away, though they rolled their eyes and trembled as Griggs approached.

"This is a stickup!" the gang leader roared. "Throw down your rifle, driver, and reach for the sky or I'll blast you to kingdom come! That goes for your passengers, too—any of you passengers who are armed better be throwin' yore pistols out the window and gettin' ready to hand over yore valuables!"

The grizzled driver complied, his arms shaking and his eyes wide. The rifle clanked as it landed against a small boulder, and there were softer, answering thuds as a Colt and a small derringer flew out the window to land in the dusty road. Thorn heard a buzz of conversation from within the coach.

"Everyone outta the coach!" Griggs ordered, and after an endless moment, the door was flung open and one by one, the passengers emerged—a rotund, balding man who looked like a drummer; a middle-aged man and wife, clutching each other fearfully; and finally, with great dignity, a silver-haired woman who had to be the wife of Simpson Creek's mayor. All of them were pale and looked terrified.

One of Griggs's men, whom Thorn knew only as Mose, rode forward, holding out a small sack. "I'll take yore valuables," he announced to the passengers.

Mrs. Gilmore began to unfasten a necklace from her throat, and the middle-aged man dug in his pocket, bringing out a pocket watch that gleamed golden in the sunlight. His wife moaned as she saw him hold it up. The drummer dropped a handful of coins into the bag.

This would be a good time for Bishop and his men to pounce, while the outlaws' attention is focused on what the passengers are handing over, Thorn thought. But there was only silence behind him, and he dared not look around, lest he give a hint of their presence.

"Is that all ya got?" Mose jeered at the passengers. "Ma'am, I think ya forgot about them gold earbobs," he said to the middle-aged woman. He gestured menacingly at her ears until she whimpered and pulled them off. "What about you, driver?" he called, and at last, the man pulled a silver flask from his trousers pocket and dropped that in with the rest of the booty.

"What about that chest up there by yore boot?" Mose demanded. "Carryin' a payroll?"

The driver shook his head, then worked the clasp and tilted the chest so that the outlaw could see it was empty. "Sorry, I already delivered that in Lampasas," he explained, with an obviously false apologetic air.

"You folks can get back inside," Tomlinson said, pointing to the coach.

Hesitatingly, darting glances back at the outlaws, the passengers began to clamber back into the coach.

"Not you, Miz Gilmore," Griggs called out, pointing his pistol at the gray-haired woman. "You'll be staying with us for a while." With his weapon, he gestured her away from the coach and her fellow passengers, to the side of the road.

Mrs. Gilmore gasped and one hand flew to her chest. "But…what do you mean? How do you know my name?"

Griggs guffawed. "We know lots o' things, Miz Gilmore—like the fact that yore husband, the mayor, is the richest man in Simpson Creek and he'll pay plenty to see you back safe 'n' sound at his side."

"You're…holding me for *ransom*?" she asked, going paler than she was before. "But—but this is an *outrage*!"

"Yeah, well, we specialize in being outrageous," Griggs said, still grinning. "I'm sure yore man'll pay up, and if you behave yoreself, no harm'll come to you and you'll be back in his arms in no time. Hold out your arms, wrists together, while one o' my boys shows you just how serious we are about this. Be quick, now!" Griggs admonished, when it looked as if the mayor's wife would like to argue further. "We'd hate to have to damage the goods... but we will if we have to. The rest of you can be on your way in just a minute."

The air had gone silent, as if the birds and even the insects were holding their breaths to see what would happen next. All Thorn could hear was the pounding of his heart, Mrs. Gilmore's indignant huffs as her wrists were tied together and the hushed murmurs of the passengers, now safely back inside the stagecoach. *Where was the posse? Was Bishop just going to let the kidnapping proceed?*

Just then he heard a thin, boyish cry, like an imitation of a rebel yell from someone who'd never heard a real one in the war, and suddenly pandemonium ensued as the sheriff and his posse charged around the bend, seemingly from out of nowhere.

"Hands up, every one of you, unless you want to die right here!" Bishop called, from the back of the lead horse. "You're under arrest!"

Thorn raised his pistol. "Do as he says—no one's getting kidnapped today. You're all under arrest."

Griggs roared in fury and leveled his pistol at the lawman. "I ain't gonna be arrested, Sheriff!" Then he turned his furious glare on Thorn. "This is your doing, Dawson, ain't it? Well, I'm gonna make you sorry—"

Bishop fired, and the outlaw leader was the first to fall, with Tomlinson the next to go down, after aiming his gun at Thorn. Pritchard dropped his Colt and raised his arms in apparent surrender, then pulled another pistol from his boot as Thorn approached to take his weapon. A shot rang out from behind them from someone in the posse and Pritchard fell from his horse. Mose and two other men tried to flee, but only one of the three succeeded in getting out of range before the posse's guns shot them off their horses.

Tense and alert, Thorn looked around to see if there were any more signs of trouble, but all the gang members were down, except for one who had been taken into custody. Mrs. Gilmore looked shaken but unharmed. And Thorn had managed to scrape by without any new bullet holes.

It was over. It was really, finally over.

"You took your sweet time about stepping in," Thorn growled at the sheriff, as Bishop stepped forward and untied Mrs. Gilmore's bonds.

"You wanted the charges to stick, didn't you?" he replied, unperturbed. "I couldn't intervene till the coach was stopped and Mrs. Gilmore was being threatened with kidnapping."

"But how could you hear that from where you were hiding?" Thorn demanded. The sheriff and his posse had to have been waiting some ways behind them on the road, or they'd have been seen.

"Didn't you hear that rebel yell?" called a familiar voice, and suddenly, from out of a patch of junipers, Billy Joe stepped forward, grinning from ear to ear. "I snuck in there after y'all arrived and waited to give the signal. Sheriff said I was to call out as soon as Mrs. Gilmore was told she was bein' kidnapped—and as soon as the passengers were safely back in the coach, on account of all the lead he figured would be flyin' around."

"But h-how…" Thorn began. "I thought you were waiting with Tilly in the cave where Mrs. Gilmore was going to be held captive."

"Miss Tilly ain't up to keepin' *me* someplace I don't wanna be," the boy crowed. "I waited till she got sleepy in the heat, then I tied her up—an' gagged her, too, so's she couldn't screech out a warning from in there. Then I snuck back, figurin' I'd help you somehow, but I found the posse first, and they told me what the plan was. I said I'd help 'em, and Sheriff Bishop told me what to do."

"And he did it exactly right," Bishop said with a grin. "Boy, I think you might have a future in law enforcement."

Chapter Fifteen

Daisy put off leaving the hotel restaurant's kitchen as long as she could. By the time she locked the door behind her, the last diner had long since paid for his supper and left, and the setting sun cast long shadows down Main Street. Returning home would only confirm its emptiness, for no one had come to tell her what had happened. Billy Joe would still be gone, and she would not know if he was alive or dead.

She wondered how the mayor was faring, waiting for his wife's return. The stagecoach that was to bring Mrs. Gilmore home was well overdue, so even if no one had let him in on the plan, he would be aware something was wrong. He had to be worrying. Should she go to him, and make sure he knew what was happening, or would that be presumptuous of her to speak of law enforcement matters without the sheriff's approval? Especially when his own wife was in danger, and Daisy had no way of knowing if the operation to protect her had ended well.

When she exited the alley and came out onto Main Street, however, Daisy saw Mayor Gilmore standing behind the wrought-iron gate in front of his mansion, holding on to it as he gazed eastward down the street in the direction the stage would come from—or the posse. Yes, he must know. When the stage hadn't come in on time, he would have inquired at the station, and when its manager could tell him nothing, he would have gone directly to the sheriff.

Impulsively, Daisy crossed the street diagonally and went to him. "Mayor Gilmore, is there any word? Have you heard…anything?"

"Good evening, Mrs. Henderson." The face he turned to her then was haggard with worry. He appeared to have aged a score of years since she had seen him last. "No, nothing since Mrs. Bishop kindly came to tell me about their planned ambush of the Griggs gang, who would be attempting to kidnap my wife," he said. "She came, since Deputy Menendez is with the posse, of course."

"I'll wait with you—if that's all right?" Suddenly, Daisy realized he might not know anything about her son being involved in this business. But if he did know that Billy Joe had run off to join the outlaws planning to abduct his wife, he'd think she had a lot of nerve.

It seemed Prissy had covered that bit of information, too, however. "That's very kind of you. Mrs. Bishop told me about your son being with…them," the mayor said, and anyone listening might have assumed he was referring to the posse rather than the outlaws, for his tone remained level. "You must be very worried."

She nodded, and wanted to say something consoling, such as, "Surely they'll all be returning soon, and we'll know everything is all right." But trying to form the words would have let loose the tears that still threatened to cascade down her cheeks.

His hand moved to the latch on the gate, and he opened it, gesturing to a stone bench a few feet away. "Come inside, Mrs. Henderson. We may as well be comfortable while we wait. We can see the street from here just as well."

She started to move forward to accept his invitation, but just then faint, far-off sounds reached her ears—the pounding of hooves and the jingling of harness, along with voices.

The sunlight was nearly gone, but even in the dimness she could make out a cluster of riders, and the dark, rolling mass of the stagecoach behind them.

She gave a little cry and pointed. "Look, Mayor Gilmore—they're coming! The posse—and the stage!"

"Thank You, God," he breathed, and they ran out beyond the fence that surrounded the mayor's property toward the procession. Daisy checked her speed out of respect for the mayor's greater age, fearful he would trip and fall in the dusty street while she ran ahead, but her eyes searched the riders, seeking the two men she loved—Thorn Dawson and her son.

She spotted Thorn first, for he rode at the front on his bay. And then, just behind him and next to Deputy Menendez, came Billy Joe, looking tired but happy. She could see one outlaw riding with the posse, his horse led by one of them—a grim-faced man with his hands tied in front. He appeared unhappy but uninjured. Was he the only outlaw who had survived?

Billy Joe spotted her first and handed the reins to the deputy, then jumped off his horse and ran toward her, not stopping until he was close enough to throw his arms around her. She threw her arms around him, too, closing her eyes in a rapture of thankfulness that he was unharmed.

"Ma! Ma, we stopped the kidnapping and captured the Griggs gang!" he cried, gesturing at the man. His face sobered. "Only one got away—all the rest of them but that one are dead, even Griggs." Billy Joe pointed behind him, and now she could see a buckboard following the stage, with a tarp covering its cargo. They must have borrowed the wagon from a nearby ranch to carry the bodies of the outlaws who had been killed.

Then Thorn was with her, too, joining in the embrace with Daisy and her son.

"Thorn, I'm so thankful to God that you're all right, you and Billy Joe," she said, glorying in the feel of his strong arms around her and her son. She felt Thorn's lips touch her forehead, and she didn't care who might be seeing it. All that mattered was that he was holding her, and both he and Billy Joe were unscathed.

It was a long moment before she could think beyond that. "Mrs. Gilmore—is she all right?"

"See for yourself," Thorn murmured, and when Daisy let go of him enough to look, she saw that the passengers of the stagecoach had spilled out into the street, and Mayor Gilmore had enfolded his wife in his arms and was kissing her with all the enthusiasm of a much younger man.

"Ma, I let the posse know when it was time to appear and capture the outlaws," Billy was saying, his face alight with the pride of accomplishment. "I had to wait till just the right moment, after the outlaws had stopped the stage and told Mrs. Gilmore she was bein' kidnapped and all." His words tumbled out with boyish excitement. "Oh, and *I* captured Miss Tilly myself!"

Startled to realize she had forgotten all about the traitorous waitress in the commotion, Daisy looked toward the riders again and this time she spotted Tilly, her hands tied in front of her just as the man's were. She was grim-faced and pale, and even looked frightened, as if she'd finally realized that allying herself with an outlaw had consequences. She'd likely serve a long prison sentence and be an old woman before she saw freedom again.

As if she felt Daisy's eyes upon her, Tilly met her gaze then, her expression hard and cold. Then she averted her face, to stare straight ahead of her. Unlike Daisy, there would be no happy ending for her, and Daisy felt a twinge of pity for her before she remembered that Tilly had made her choices—choices that included trying to take away Daisy's son. She would pray for her, Daisy decided, but that was all she could do.

"Sheriff Bishop says your boy's a hero, Daisy," Thorn said.

"Yeah, an' he says I got a future in law enforcement," Billy Joe told her proudly.

Daisy blinked in amazement, thinking it a generous remark from Bishop, under the circumstances. It certainly represented an amazing transformation in a boy who only weeks ago had aspired to be an outlaw. "That would be mighty fine, Billy Joe."

"Ma, is there anything at the house for supper? I'm starved," Billy Joe said. "We ain't eaten all day." As if to confirm his words, his stomach growled loudly.

"We *haven't* eaten, you mean," Daisy corrected automatically, hoping her chickens in the barn would be willing to part with some eggs. But perhaps there was a better option…

While they had been talking, the mayor and his wife had turned and walked back to their home, and Deputy Menendez had assisted the sheriff to escort the prisoners to the nearby jail. The rest of the posse had gone home, too. Now Daisy, Thorn and Billy Joe stood alone in the growing darkness on Main Street. The only lights showing were those of the saloon and the hotel, opposite each other just down the street.

"Come to the hotel," she said. "I reckon I can rustle up a good supper for y'all there."

Billy Joe's mouth dropped open. "But Ma, the restaurant's closed for the night, ain't—*isn't* it? Won't you get in trouble with Mr. Prendergast?"

Now it was Daisy's turn to grin. "If he minds me cooking up some vittles for a couple of heroes, he can fire me."

Mr. Prendergast said nothing the next morning about the impromptu late dinner she had made after the restaurant was closed. It was likely he had been fast asleep in his room upstairs by that time, and never even knew it had happened, but Daisy made sure to put money for their meals in with the day's receipts.

When she returned home the following night from work, Thorn was waiting for her in the kitchen along with Billy Joe. "Sheriff Bishop sent a telegraph to the State Police headquarters confirming my role in the capture of the Griggs gang, and they've already replied. I have to go to Austin tomorrow and collect my reward."

Daisy suppressed a wince of dismay. "How far is that—at least a two days' ride, isn't it? So you'll be gone almost a week?" She tried to sound strong and matter-of-fact about it, but now that he was no longer in danger and there was no reason to hide their relationship, she didn't want him to leave, even for a short time.

"The telegraph also mentioned something about a promotion, and a meeting with the governor, so I might have to stay there a few days before I can head back."

She put a hand to her mouth now, feeling tears stinging her eyes. The State Police were going to try to lure him into staying with them, she just knew it, and if they succeeded, he and Daisy would never have their ranch near Mason. And Thorn might meet ladies in Austin who were far more alluring than small-town Daisy Henderson.

He reached a hand across the table to touch hers. "I've got to go so we can get our ranch up and running, sweetheart. I'll be back as soon as I can, you know that."

Our ranch, he'd said. His calling it "ours" resonated warmly in her heart. But she still had one fear. He'd conquered one pack of outlaws, but there were still plenty roaming Texas. "On your way back, I...

I don't like to think of you riding alone, carrying a large sum of cash, Thorn…"

Billy Joe had been watching them quietly as they talked, but now he protested. "Ma, Thorn just defeated the whole Griggs gang—*practic'ly* single-handed! I reckon riding to Austin and back's no big thing for him, no matter what two-bit outlaws he'd meet up with."

She saw Thorn suppress a smile. "Billy Joe, I don't want you thinking of me as some superhuman fellow. Taking down the Griggs gang would have been impossible on my own—it took the cooperation of brave men like yourself. You know that, right?" Daisy saw him make eye contact with her son.

Billy Joe glanced away first. "Yes, sir."

Now Thorn looked at her. "And don't you worry, Daisy. I'd already thought of that, and I'll make arrangements with a bank in Austin to wire the money to the Simpson Creek branch, so there won't be any bags of cash weighing me down, or making me look like a good target to someone considering a holdup."

She made an effort to collect herself, so that when her eyes met his, she was smiling bravely. "All right, that sounds better. I know you'll come back as soon as you can." She wanted him to know she was as eager as he was to start their new life, even though it meant leaving Simpson Creek.

She saw her son suppress a yawn and realized

how late it was getting. "Billy Joe, take the sheets I laundered out to the barn for Thorn's cot, please."

But Thorn shook his head. "No, I'm sleeping at the hotel tonight. Now that the whole town knows what happened and that you and I are courting, Daisy, I think it's best that we give the gossips nothing to wag their tongues about. I'll be by come sunup to collect Ace, though, so we can say our goodbyes then."

Again she was touched by his thoughtfulness for her reputation. Mrs. Donahue, her nosy neighbor, had made it a point to quiz her about her "Ranger-in-disguise sweetheart," as she called him. The woman would probably be peeking out her back window, which faced the Henderson barn, to see whether or not he left for the night.

Billy Joe could be thoughtful, too, for now he stood and extended his hand to Thorn. "Good night, then, Mr. Thorn. I'll see you in the morning." After the two had shaken hands, the boy left the kitchen, and Daisy heard his bedroom door creak open before it was firmly shut.

He had left them alone. "He…he's growing up, isn't he?" she commented, looking in the direction Billy Joe had gone.

"Yes, he is. He's going to be a fine man, Daisy—a credit to you."

Her throat felt thick with pride. She'd better get herself together or she'd waste this moment crying like a baby, she thought.

Thorn knelt by where she was sitting, then cleared his throat and took her hand. His eyes shone in the lamplight.

"Daisy, I love you, and I'm ready to make a life with you—you and Billy Joe. You reckon by the time I come back, you'd be ready to marry me?"

It wasn't a fancy proposal, she thought, even if he *was* kneeling, but it wasn't in her to be coy and pretend she hadn't already understood the depth of his caring for her, and that he wanted to make it permanent. Nor could she pretend that her feelings didn't match his. She loved him, and she wanted to spend the rest of her life with him.

She nodded, feeling as if the glowing lamp matched the glowing happiness within her. "The Spinsters Club has already promised to help me plan the wedding," she said, already thinking about what she might wear. She could ride out to Milly Brookfield's ranch, for the founder of the Spinsters Club was well known around Simpson Creek for speedily made, beautiful gowns. She'd have to take a day off work, and Mr. Prendergast wouldn't be happy about that, but he'd soon have to get used to doing without her entirely, wouldn't he?

"Will it be hard for you to leave Simpson Creek, Daisy?" Thorn asked.

She thought about her answer for a moment. "In some ways," she said, nodding. "There are such good people here. Folks who have helped me and stood by me in many ways." Simpson Creek had been the scene of so much that had happened to her, good and bad—her childhood, her marriage, the birth of her son, the sense of shame she'd lived with for so long after she'd discovered what an awful man her first husband was and the renewal of her self-worth as the women of the Spinsters Club came alongside her to support her when her husband was arrested, jailed and later killed in prison.

"But there are good women in Mason, too, aren't there?" she asked. "Your sisters…"

He nodded. "We'll make sure to get into town regularly so you can meet them and the other ladies there, as well as go to church. I think the congregation has a Ladies Aid Society. My sisters always seemed to have a fine time at their events."

"Thorn, I'll miss Simpson Creek, but I'm not worried about leaving. Anywhere I am with you will be home."

"Then I think we should seal the deal with a kiss," he said, and gathered her into his arms.

Chapter Sixteen

If it hadn't been for nighttime, Daisy would have been almost too busy to miss Thorn. Mr. Prendergast had been in such a dither when he learned that Tilly, the waitress he had treated with such favoritism, was not only awaiting trial in the Simpson Creek jail, but likely a lengthy prison sentence, as well. Pitying the man, Daisy hadn't had the heart to tell him that she would also be quitting as cook as soon as Thorn returned from Austin and their wedding took place. Instead, she called an emergency meeting of the Spinsters Club in the late afternoon, when the restaurant normally had little business, to see if any of the Spinsters could serve as a waitress, at least until other arrangements could be made.

To her great relief, Jane Jeffries, a single mother and widow who was the only one of the original Spinsters Club members who had not made a match, raised her hand to volunteer. Daisy could have hugged her out of sheer relief, but not wanting to overwhelm the woman, settled for merely thanking her and asking if she could start tomorrow.

"I… I'd like to," Jane replied, looking like a deer that had just been startled from a mesquite thicket. "I've been needing to earn some money to supplement my late husband's soldier's pension, but what will I do with Calvin until school starts up in the fall again? He's such a lively boy…he's ten, you know, but I don't know how well he'd do on his own for several hours a day…"

If my Billy Joe can do it, Calvin can, Daisy thought tartly, but before she could say so, she remembered how often being on his own had led Billy Joe into trouble and bad habits. He might not have fallen in with troublemaking friends or developed the admiration for outlaws that had so nearly been his undoing if she'd been able to stay at home and keep an eye on him, so she ought to be more sympathetic to Jane's plight. Perhaps she should volunteer Billy Joe to watch over Jane's son. His behavior was excellent now—surely he could be a role model for Jane's "lively" son.

Then she remembered his daily job at Ella's café. There wasn't enough work for both boys to do, and from what Daisy had seen of Jane Jeffries's son, labeling him as "lively" was a charitable description at best. It wasn't fair to expect Ella Bohannan and Billy Joe to keep Calvin Jeffries out of trouble.

The silence lengthened and Daisy was afraid Jane would have to bow out of her waitressing job before she had even begun it, but then Sarah Walker spoke up.

"Let me speak with my husband," she said. "He's been talking about how he'd like to have an apprentice to help him with his doctoring. I used to do that, but with our growing family…" She laid a hand over her midsection and blushed.

"Sarah! Are you saying you're expecting again?" cried Milly with delight, and her sister nodded. "How wonderful!"

The meeting dispersed soon after that, with Sarah promising to speak to her husband about Calvin as soon as she got home, and then coming to tell Daisy what he'd said.

"I'm really thankful you think you can help me at the restaurant, Jane," Daisy said as they put the dining room back in order.

Jane gave her a shy, genuine smile. "It'll be good to get out and be earning some money, Daisy. You're sure I can do this—keep it straight who ordered what, and carry the dishes without dropping them?"

Daisy laughed. "Of course you can. You'll do fine," she said with an encouraging smile. "It'll be good to have you there." She'd have to have a talk with her later about not letting Mr. Prendergast bully her, but she didn't want to frighten her away before she even started work.

"Yes…well, I'd better hurry on home," Jane murmured, and rushed out of the restaurant as if she feared Calvin was burning their house down in her absence.

So she'd taken care of the waitress problem, assuming Dr. Walker consented to take on Calvin as his apprentice, Daisy thought as she returned to the hotel kitchen. Hopefully, finding someone to take over her job would be just as easy. Perhaps Mayor Gilmore's delightful Mexican cook, Flora, had a relative who wanted to be a hotel cook? Daisy would see that everything was taken care of and all the loose ends tied up…and then she'd be ready to start her new life with Thorn.

"Ma, when's Thorn coming home?" Billy Joe asked several days later, as she warmed up the leftovers that she'd brought home from work for their supper. "I miss him." His face was wistful.

Daisy sighed. "So do I, son. And I'm not sure— he left a week ago, and it'd take him two days' riding at least to get to Austin, if all went well, and the same to return. But he had business to take care of in Austin that he thought might keep him in town for several days, and that's what we don't know—how long it will take to report to the headquarters of the State Police, and speak to the governor."

"I bet he's being celebrated as a hero," Billy Joe said, eyes alight. "Maybe they're even staging a parade in his honor!"

Daisy had to smile at her son's enthusiasm. It was more fun to think of Thorn being honored for his heroism than it was to follow her own self-doubts, picturing Thorn being offered such a choice job in the State Police that he couldn't turn it down, so he'd never return to Simpson Creek. Or that perhaps some lovely Austin girl had caught his eye, one who was younger and not burdened with a child already... Daisy was supposed to ride out to Milly's ranch tomorrow afternoon to discuss the dress her friend had agreed to make for her wedding. Perhaps she should wait until Thorn actually returned. She'd feel like a fool having spent good money on a gown if—

Stop it, Daisy, she told herself. Thorn was a trustworthy man, and she could believe in his love for her and that he would do what he'd said he would do. There was no reason for her to feel so insecure. She was just tired.

She wondered what Thorn would wear if—no, *when* he married her. Except for when he'd been disguising himself as a preacher in a frock coat and fine trousers, she'd never seen him in anything but denim trousers and a shirt and sometimes a leather vest. If he dressed himself in fancy clothes for their wedding, would she feel as if she was marrying Reverend Dinwiddy instead of Thorn Dawson? But it didn't matter what clothes he turned up in for their wedding, she thought. He would look handsome in anything.

"Ma, I think when I grow up, I want to be a Texas Ranger, just like Thorn."

Her heart gave a little leap of pride mingled with apprehension. It was an honorable ambition, and one Billy Joe might not have had if Thorn Dawson had not happened into their barn when he'd been wounded. But was she a strong enough mother to let her son court danger the way Thorn had?

That's many years from now, she reminded herself. *Years in which he can—and likely will—change his mind about what he wants to be a dozen times over. And if this ambition lasts and he truly does follow this path, then, when the time comes, you won't want to cripple your son with your motherly fears.*

"But Thorn isn't a Texas Ranger," she reminded Billy Joe. "At least, he can't call himself that. The Reconstruction government dissolved the Texas Rangers because of the War Between the States."

"I wouldn't want to be a state policeman," her son said. "But Thorn says they'll be called Texas Rangers again someday soon. They just gotta get that carpetbag government out of Austin first."

Daisy sighed. Texas had been under military control until just this year, when E. J. Davis, the carpetbag candidate, as Texans called him, had taken office. It would be a while till he and others like him could be voted out, she assumed. "It's all in God's hands, Billy Joe. Maybe you could add that to your nighttime prayers. And speaking of which—"

"I know, I know. It's bedtime. G'night, Ma."

She would do well to follow her own advice, Daisy thought. Thorn's return, and their future, were both in God's hands, so she would pray about them when she went to bed tonight and waited to fall asleep. But she knew she wouldn't take an easy breath until she saw Thorn again.

Thorn's heart lifted as he reined Ace onto the road that led northwest out of Austin. He was going home—home to Simpson Creek, to Daisy and Billy Joe. It felt good to have a place that he thought of as home again. He hadn't had one for most of his adult years.

If he ever had to return to the state capital it would be too soon, he thought. He never again wanted to see Austin controlled by a puppet government. He could now say he'd met the governor. E. J. Davis was a genial enough sort, but it seemed like no great honor to have met him, since he hadn't won his seat in government through hard work or the goodwill of the people of Texas. Instead, he'd been handpicked to run for the office and guaranteed to win it by the federals who still truly controlled Texas.

Only now that Thorn had spent some time in Austin was he fully aware of how corrupt the State Police were, how completely a tool of the carpetbag government and the crooked head of the force, James Davidson. They'd done little to keep the peace except to suppress the Ku Klux Klan, and outlaws who were arrested were often "shot during an attempted escape" rather than brought to justice. It was easier to do it that way, and no officer had to fear any consequences for his actions when there was no real responsible oversight.

They'd certainly tried to keep Thorn on the force, with Captain Hepplewhite offering to make him a sergeant if he'd sign back on for an immediate placement, with a captaincy promised if he'd pledge to stay another year.

But all Thorn had to do was think of Daisy, and it was easy to politely decline.

They'd kept him in Austin a week, delaying his meeting with the governor deliberately, he thought, to give him time to reconsider. Meanwhile they'd treated him like royalty, accompanying him to the best restaurants, introducing him to the daughters of politicians and officers in the State Police hierarchy, to show Thorn he could have a rich, lavish life if he stayed. And all it would cost him would be his conscience and his self-respect. Despite all the glittering elegance, it just made him more eager to shake the dust of Austin off his feet and return to the simplicity and honesty of Simpson Creek. He smiled, remembering something he'd purchased that now traveled, neatly folded, in his saddlebags. He was certain Daisy would think he had made good use of his free time in Austin.

All things considered, he was glad to look down at his chest and no longer see the tin star of the State Police resting there. Someday, please God, the Texas Rangers would ride again, and a man could be proud to say he was one of them. But until then, Thorn could be proud of the accomplishments that he had in store—being a good husband to Daisy and a good father to Billy Joe.

It was nearly closing time and Daisy was eyeing the beef stew remaining in the pot on the stove. Business had been slow today, with few travelers passing through, few ranchers coming to town and most locals choosing to stay at home due to the heat. August in Texas was hot as election day in a hornet's nest, old Delbert Turner had said at noon, when he'd come in for some lemonade, so maybe beef stew hadn't been a good choice to make. But few customers meant that there would be more than enough of the stew to divide, sending half home with Jane, and taking the rest for herself and Billy Joe, in case her son had not brought leftovers home from Ella's café.

Asking Jane Jeffries to take the waitressing job had been a wise move on Daisy's part. Even Mr. Prendergast, who handed out compliments less often than cows gave whiskey, agreed. She was cheerful and efficient, and never flirted with the male customers as Tilly had. She was gaining in confidence, too, and had lost the frightened-deer look she'd had when Daisy first asked her to consider the job.

Jane came into the kitchen just then. "Do you think we dare put the Closed sign on the door yet? It'd be five minutes early, but the streets were empty last I looked…" Her face was wistful, and Daisy knew Jane was as tired as she was, and wanted to pick up her son from the doctor's home.

"Better not," Daisy said, rolling her eyes. "Even though Mr. Prendergast's already been here for his supper, it'd be just like him to stroll downstairs again to check up on us. But watch the clock over the stove, and as soon as it's time—"

A faint tinkle at the door reached their ears just then, the sound of the little bell over the door that announced new customers.

In unison, the two women groaned.

"I shouldn't have said anything—I jinxed us," Jane said ruefully.

"Now, now, you're not superstitious, are you?" Daisy retorted. "Better go welcome them. Tell them all we have left is beef stew, though." At least she wouldn't have to take the remainder—whatever couldn't be carried home by her or Jane—down to the storage area in the cellar, she thought. She disliked going down there at night, even with the brightest of lanterns, after hearing that one of the victims of the infamous Comanche raid years ago had taken refuge down there and died of his wounds. *Now who was being superstitious?*

She resisted an urge to peek out through the pass-through window to see how many customers she would need to heat up beef stew for. Jane would be back soon enough to tell her. Daisy just hoped it wouldn't be someone with an aversion to beef stew. She could offer them bacon and eggs, which could be prepared quickly, but that was as far as she was willing to go for someone inconsiderate enough to come right at closing time and expect a full selection.

Then she chided herself for her unwilling spirit. It might be a traveler, weary and hungry, who had traveled all day and had just reached Simpson Creek. What if another cook between here and Austin treated Thorn so coldly?

The swinging door creaked, and Jane was back. "It's just a man and a boy," she announced, "but they want to see you first." She was smiling, which Daisy found odd under the circumstances.

"Why? Does the boy want me to serve his stew without carrots?" Daisy asked, making a wry face. Billy Joe used to refuse to eat carrots when he was little, she remembered. She hadn't minded leaving them out of a stew, but such an accommodation had enraged his father…

"No-o-o…" Jane said. "Go see them."

Now Daisy noticed the sparkle in her eyes, as if the other woman knew a delightful secret.

Could it possibly be—? She hurried through the door.

It was! Thorn sat there at the middle table, dusty and travel-stained, but his grin was as wide as that of the boy who sat beside him. There was no star on Thorn's shirt.

"Look who's home, Ma!" Billy Joe crowed. "We came to surprise you!"

Daisy startled everyone in the restaurant by her shriek of joy. *He'd come back, he'd actually come back!* Suddenly all her fears that Thorn wouldn't return, that he'd stay with the police and forget all about his promises of a life with her and Billy Joe, seemed so silly. *Why had she doubted him for a single second?*

The dark eyes that met hers were full of love— they weren't the eyes of a man who made empty promises. She was in his strong arms in an instant, her lips meeting his with urgent force, as if she could hardly believe he was real. He tasted salty and still smelled of his horse, but she couldn't imagine anything better than his kiss.

After Thorn and Billy Joe were full of beef stew, Thorn walked them home, though he was again taking a room at the hotel.

"I suppose you have to work tomorrow?" he asked Daisy as they strolled down the darkened main street toward her house. He wanted to ask her how soon she could quit her job—right now wasn't too soon for him, because he wanted nothing more than to spend all his time with the woman he loved. He didn't want to be unreasonable, though, and knew Daisy was too conscientious to be inconsiderate of her employer.

"No. But I do have plans..." she said, her eyes dancing.

"Plans? But I don't want to let you out of my sight, woman," he protested mock-indignantly, and smiled at Billy Joe's chuckle. "I rode all the way from Austin like Ace's tail was on fire just to hurry back to your side, and you tell me you have *plans?*"

"Yes, but as long as you don't mind riding out to the Brookfields' ranch with me, you can come, too," she told him.

"Sure, we can do that. Why don't we rent a buggy at the livery, and I'll let Ace rest in your barn. But why are you going out there?"

"It just so happens Milly's making me a dress," she told him, smiling as her voice trailed off mysteriously, and then he caught on.

"She's making you a dress? Is there a special occasion coming up?" He grinned down at her, loving the way her deep-set blue eyes gleamed.

"*Maybe*... And she's ready to do a final fitting on the dress she's been making for me. But you can't see it yet," she told him with mock severity.

Thorn pretended to look disappointed. "I understand her husband's quite the cattleman. I suppose I could pick up some pointers from him about ranching, seeing as I'm about to change professions..."

"I don't hafta go, do I?" Billy Joe asked.

"You don't want to go?" Daisy asked, surprised. He'd always been eager to go out to the ranch, where he could ride a horse and learn roping tricks from the cowboys.

He shrugged. "Miss Ella's dependin' on me at her café," he said. "And besides, you and Thorn'll probably want to do more of that *kissing* stuff on the way there and back," he said, rolling his eyes in pretended disgust.

Daisy couldn't smother her laughter. Her little boy wasn't a little boy anymore, but he still wanted to disguise his thoughtfulness as something else. She was glad he didn't seem to mind sharing her with Thorn.

"All right then—we probably won't be home till late evening. You could stop in at the hotel for your supper. I'll ask Jane to save you something. Senora Flora from the mayor's house is going to be doing the cooking at the restaurant tomorrow."

"Yippee! I hope she makes tamales!" The Mexican housekeeper had contributed them to a church supper some time ago, and Billy Joe had never forgotten.

They'd have so many more good memories now, Daisy realized. Life would be full of happy occasions, and home would be a place filled with the people they loved best. She remembered when she'd been married to William and had dreaded waking up every day.

There's no more reason for me to fear for the future, she realized. *Now I can't wait for the rest of my life to begin.*

"You're sure the Spinsters Club would be ready to hold the wedding reception in just two weeks? That wouldn't be rushing y'all too much?" Daisy asked doubtfully, looking down at Milly from the chair she was standing on while Milly pinned the hem of her wedding dress.

Milly had a mouthful of pins held at the ready, but she spit them out into her hand before replying. "Of course we'll be ready. We started making plans at the last meeting, when we knew for sure that you and Thorn were in love—how to decorate the church, who's cooking what for the reception afterward… and Reverend Chadwick was out to visit yesterday, so I know for a fact there's no other wedding scheduled for two weeks from now on Saturday. And the hem's the only thing left to do on this dress," she added, holding the fabric between her hands as she expertly placed the pins.

"I think it's the finest wedding dress you've ever made, and I've seen several of yours," Daisy said, remembering other Spinsters Club marriages. She stared down at the ivory mousseline de soie creation that fitted her to perfection now that Milly had made

a few nips and tucks here and there. It was simple
and elegant, with a diamond-shaped neckline, lace
trim only at the edge of the scalloped bishop sleeves
and along the hem, with satin trim banding on the
lower skirt and the belted waist. The gown featured
a bustle and an elegant train—a short one, but it
made Daisy feel like a princess who was about to
marry her prince.

"Thank you," Milly said, beaming with pleasure.
"It's for sure I've never seen a happier bride. Nick
and I are so pleased for you and Thorn, Daisy. And
what is the groom wearing?" She nodded toward
the parlor's high window. It looked out on the back
porch, and through it, they could hear the low hum
of conversation from Milly's husband and Thorn as
they discussed the finer points of the cattle business.

Daisy shrugged. "I don't know. He's being very
mysterious about that. He tells me not to worry my
pretty little head about it."

Milly chuckled. "Men! When Nick and I married,
he wore a suit that had been made by his London
tailor, since he hadn't been in America that long,"
she said. "Since then, though, it takes a wedding or
a Sunday church service for me to see him in anything but dusty ranch clothes. But since I love him
no matter what he wears, it doesn't really make much
of a difference. I haven't known your Thorn for long,
but from what I've seen of him—and the way you
look at him—he'll be more than presentable come

your wedding day, whatever he wears, at least as far as you're concerned. Oh my, it's noon already," she added, when the grandfather clock in the parlor began to chime the hour. She set the last pin in place. "Hop down from there and change your clothes, and we'll get a meal together."

Warmed by her friend's approval, Daisy changed back into the clothes she'd worn for the trip to the ranch. Surely good friends were almost as big a blessing as the love of a good man.

Chapter Seventeen

The heat of the day had faded somewhat by the time Thorn and Daisy headed back to her house in Simpson Creek.

"So we'll be married in two weeks?" Thorn said, after Daisy told him about what she and Milly had discussed. "That's wonderful, sweetheart. It can't come too soon for me."

Daisy nodded, pleased by his eagerness. "Milly's going to bring the dress the day before, when she comes into town to help decorate the church, and the social hall for the reception. And Billy Joe's going to stay with them while we take our wedding trip out to your ranch—"

"*Our* ranch," he corrected her with a grin. Then, noticing her smile fade, he asked, "What's wrong, sweetheart? Don't you want to move there anymore?"

Once again, she'd been transparent. If he had

acted angry or hurt at her reaction, she might have hesitated to answer him, but his gaze was clear and honest, his expression encouraging her to share her heart with him.

"Oh, no, Thorn, it's just that…didn't you say that your oldest sister and her husband and family have been living in the main ranch house?" When he nodded, she went on. "I just feel uncomfortable about displacing them, that's all…"

He put out a hand to touch her wrist. "Daisy, Ellanora and Hap have always told me that when I'm ready to quit being a Ranger and settle down at the ranch, they'd be ready to move out, and the last letter I got from them, just the other day, confirms that. Ellanora's older than me, you know, and has raised a passel of kids, and now those kids are almost all grown and gone, starting their own lives nearby. So Ellanora's been feeling like the big ranch house is too much room for just her and Hap. Now, I'm planning to offer Hap the foremanship of the ranch, if he wants it—and I think he will—until Billy Joe's old enough to take over, at least. Would you mind if I spent part of our honeymoon building them a small house on the ranch property, close to ours but far enough apart that you and Ellanora can run your own households? I think we could do it, Hap and me, and if I know the family, most of them will turn out to help us build it, along with the ranch hands."

He'd thought of everything, Daisy realized. She'd

been about to say she and Thorn and his sister and
her husband could share the big ranch house, but
such an arrangement never would have worked for
long, especially when one of the women had been accustomed to being mistress of the house prior to the
second woman's coming. Daisy imagined watching
Thorn build a house during the day while she and
his sister cooked the builders hearty meals for their
midday breaks, and the evenings she would spend
with her new husband...

She murmured, "That sounds perfect, Thorn. I
can't wait to meet your sister and the rest of your
family."

He squeezed her fingers before returning his right
hand to the reins. "You're a good woman, Daisy Henderson. I can't wait until you're Daisy Dawson."

"Me, neither. It has a nice ring to it, doesn't it?"
she said, and then it seemed the perfect time for one
of those kissing stops that Billy Joe professed to be
so embarrassed about.

"Are you happy?" Thorn asked her a few minutes
later, after he'd kissed her for a long while that still
wasn't nearly long enough.

She nodded. "I didn't think it was possible to be
this happy, Thorn." It was true, she *was* happier than
she'd ever thought of being. But realizing how happy
she was just made her remember someone else who
could not possibly be happy at this time.

"Then why do your eyes look troubled?"

Would she ever learn how not to show every thought in her head?

"I *am* happy, Thorn, unbelievably happy—but I keep thinking of Tilly in that jail cell. She'll be in prison for a long time, won't she?"

His face sobered and he nodded. "It's likely. Don't you think she's earned it, for helping Griggs as she did? If things had gone the way that she'd planned, Mrs. Gilmore would have been held for ransom and possibly killed."

Daisy nodded. "Yes, of course. It just feels wrong to be so happy when her future is so…so bleak."

He put his arm around her and hugged her, then kissed her cheek. "I'll say it again, Daisy, you're a good woman. You know Tilly wouldn't spare a thought for you if your positions were reversed."

He was right, Daisy knew, but she also knew she wouldn't be completely at peace if she ignored the urging in her heart. Wasn't there a verse in the Scriptures that said "I was in prison, and you visited Me," meaning it was the same as doing it for Jesus himself?

"I know. But she's got to be feeling so alone, with Griggs dead, knowing she'll stand trial soon. I think I'll go see her, between now and the trial. See if I can…somehow be a friend to her." The trial was scheduled to start next week, when the circuit judge could be in Simpson Creek. It would probably be a quick affair, over well before their wedding.

"You're an amazing woman, Daisy," Thorn told her. "I don't know why God thought I was worthy of you, but I'm blessed that He did."

"What are you doing here? Come to gloat, did you?"

The woman who faced her from the other side of the bars and taunted her as she approached appeared to have aged ten years at least since Daisy had last seen her. She wore a baggy dress of a coarse, plain fabric that Daisy knew she would have scorned to wear before she'd been arrested. She'd always put such stock in looking pretty and fashionable, wanting to be admired and desired by every man she met.

Gone was the bravado and the lively flirtatiousness that had been the essence of Tilly Pridemore. *Pride no more*, thought Daisy.

Her throat felt thick as she tried to find the right words. "No, I haven't come to gloat, Tilly. I... I just wanted to see how you were, and if you needed anything."

The woman turned to the man in the next cell, the other outlaw who had been captured with her, and chuckled. "Mose, she wants to know if I need anything."

The other outlaw guffawed. "Why don't you tell her you'd like to borrow that big key ring the sheriff keeps in his desk, the one that would let both of us out of these cells? You sure could use that. Oh, and a coupla horses we could ride away on, as long as she's asking."

Tilly grinned, but there was no warmth in it, just a stretching of her lips in a mockery of a smile. She turned back to Daisy. "Well?"

"You know I can't do that," Daisy said. "And maybe you don't want to hear this, but I wanted you to know I forgive you, Tilly, for what you did."

The words seemed to hang there in the air between the two of them.

Tilly blinked, and her mouth fell open for a moment.

"If that don't beat all," she said. "'Spose you could tell the judge how you feel, and he'll forget about sending me to prison?"

But Daisy felt no urge to rise to the bait. "You and I both know I can't change that, Tilly. But maybe I could write to you, while you're in prison. You told me once you don't have any family. And you won't be in there forever... When you get released, you could come out to the ranch where we'll be living, if you want. The Dancing D, it's called, north of Mason a few miles. We could give you work..."

She thought it likely that Tilly would jeer at that, but if the woman had truly thought about what she would do when her prison sentence was done, she'd have to have realized her options would be severely limited. Decent folks would shun her if they knew she'd served time. Unless she traveled many miles and lied about her background, there would be little open to her but jobs so menial Tilly might be tempted into lawbreaking again, or prostitution— and she would be too old by then to be very appealing as a soiled dove.

"You oughta be smart an' take her up on it, Tilly," Mose muttered from the far cell. "You ain't gonna be gettin' many nice offers like that, you know."

Tilly was still staring at her as if she couldn't believe her ears. "Well, I'll be jiggered," she murmured, shaking her head. "You really mean it, don't you? Does that handsome husband-to-be of yours know you're offering a jailbird a job?"

Daisy nodded, and didn't mention the fact that Thorn had warned her Tilly would probably laugh in her face at such an offer. "He said it was okay."

"And what would *I* do on a ranch, Daisy Henderson?" Tilly retorted, cynicism gleaming from her hard eyes. "Round up longhorns with the rest of the cowpunchers?"

Daisy shrugged. "From what I hear, the woman who cooks for the ranch hands is getting along in years. You always wanted to be a cook, didn't you? I can't think of a better audience for your culinary skills than a bunch of cowboys…"

Daisy could see Tilly was turning it over in her

mind, imagining it. The idea of cooking for men had to appeal to her, but Tilly also had to know she'd be a lot older by then, not to mention worn down by the harshness of years of prison life—hardly someone the cowboys would flirt with.

"We'll see," she said at last. "I don't even know how many years off that'll be yet, before I can take you up on such an offer. Why did you make it— and why forgive me, if you don't mind me asking? It seems like you've got it made—you're about to marry a handsome hero and go off to a peachy new life as Thorn Dawson's wife. You're shaking the dust of this town off your boots. It would be easy for you to leave it all behind—and especially to leave *me* behind. It's not like we were ever friends, and you don't owe me a thing. Why do you need to be asking for any more trouble?"

Daisy took a deep breath before replying. "Because I'm a Christian, Tilly. The Bible instructs us to forgive and offer help."

The woman whistled. "All those Sunday mornings you took off work to go to church taught you that? I thought you were wasting your time, but I guess not."

Daisy nodded. "I learned a lot from Reverend Chadwick's sermons and reading my Bible."

Tilly looked wistful. "I never did have a Bible, but I didn't have much book learning, neither, though

I can read and write enough to get by. Reckon I couldn't understand the Good Book, though."

Daisy hadn't dreamed she'd be offered such an open door by Tilly, but saying a quick silent "thank You" to God, she walked right through it. Reaching inside her reticule, she pulled out the New Testament she used to read on her breaks. "I think you could, Tilly, if you give it a try. I want you to have this."

The woman's eyes widened as she recognized the book she'd often caught Daisy reading. "Oh, no, I couldn't—not your Bible, Daisy."

"This is just the New Testament, Tilly. My family Bible—with the Old and New Testament—is at home, so I'll still have one to read, too. Please take this one. Start with the Gospels—they're right at the beginning. If you pray and read it, it will give you hope—I promise it will."

Want struggled with pride in the other woman's eyes, but at last she reached a hand through the bars and took the leather-bound volume. "Guess I'll be having some time to read, that's for sure, and I'll need all the hope I can get. Thank you, Daisy. You're better to me than I deserve."

Daisy felt tears stinging her eyes, even as peace settled over her heart. "You're welcome, Tilly. I have to go now, but I'll visit again."

"I'd like that."

Daisy left the jail then, knowing she had a shift to

finish at the restaurant, but her heart felt so light it might well float away. She couldn't wait to tell Thorn and Billy Joe about her time with Tilly.

Everything was in readiness. The pews were packed with what looked like the entire population of Simpson Creek. The mayor and his wife were there, with Mrs. Gilmore looking none the worse for her recent abduction. Mrs. Detwiler, the matron who was the social arbiter of Simpson Creek, was present, as were all the Spinsters Club members. Thorn's sisters and their families had made the trek from Mason to welcome her into the family, and she was looking forward to getting to know them better. A couple of Thorn's Ranger compadres had come, too. Wonder of wonders, Mr. Prendergast had even closed the hotel restaurant for several hours, ostensibly so that he could attend, but also because he knew no one in town would be anywhere else but at this church, seeing Daisy Henderson wedding Thorn Dawson.

The Spinsters Club had decorated the ends of the pews with sunflowers, the only blossoms still plentifully in the late summer Texas sunshine. But Daisy's bouquet was made up of—what else?—daisies, grown in Mrs. Detwiler's greenhouse, mixed with some creamy ivory roses that matched the hue of her mousseline de soie bridal dress beautifully.

Billy Joe, wearing his new Sunday-best suit and

proud as a peacock in full bloom that his mother had picked him to walk her down the aisle, wore a daisy as his boutonniere. Standing at the altar was Sheriff Bishop, Thorn's best man, with Dr. Walker serving as his other groomsman. Milly and Prissy, carrying sunflowers, attended Daisy as dual matrons of honor.

And now, as she drew near to the altar where Thorn waited for her, she saw why she needn't have worried about what he would wear to their wedding. He had on a new frock coat of an elegant black fabric, with an ivory paisley silk cravat rather than the string tie she would have expected. He wore an ivory rosebud as his boutonniere.

How devastatingly handsome could one man be? How had he managed to obtain such a stylish suit in Simpson Creek, one of the smallest towns in Texas? For a certainty, he didn't buy it at the mercantile, nor would Milly, even if she had the ability, have had time to make it for him, what with his long absence in Austin.

He must have bought it in Austin, Daisy guessed. The finest tailors in Texas had their shops in the state capital, so that the wealthy and powerful figures of government could be clothed at the height of fashion.

The fact that Thorn had taken the time to be fitted for such a well-designed suit, looking forward to their wedding and planning ahead for that day, when he had been busy dealing with so many details about his future, touched her heart. It might be years before he would need to dress so stylishly again, but he had known it would please her on this special day, so he had taken the time and the trouble.

And then Daisy and her son reached Thorn's side, and Billy Joe was handing her over to her groom. Reverend Gil Chadwick was murmuring the age-old words, "Dearly beloved, we are gathered here today…"

* * * * *

Don't miss these other
BRIDES OF SIMPSON CREEK *stories*
from Laurie Kingery:
Small-town Texas spinsters find love
with mail-order grooms!

MAIL ORDER COWBOY
THE DOCTOR TAKES A WIFE
THE SHERIFF'S SWEETHEART
THE RANCHER'S COURTSHIP
THE PREACHER'S BRIDE
HILL COUNTRY CATTLEMAN
A HERO IN THE MAKING
HILL COUNTRY COURTSHIP

Find more great reads at www.Harlequin.com.

Dear Reader,

Thanks for choosing *Lawman in Disguise.* I hope you enjoyed reading about Thorn and Daisy's journey to love. My favorite heroes are like Thorn— tough, but not so much so that they don't want to serve as good role models to troubled boys like Billy Joe, and wanting to make a better life with a woman who has known only hard work and the disappointment of a previous brutal husband. In my other job, as an ER nurse, I see too many abused women and find myself hoping and praying for a happily-ever-after for each of them.

As a native Texan, I find Texas history is dear to me, especially the beautiful Hill Country, though I live elsewhere now. The Reconstruction period after the Civil War was a particularly difficult time in Texas history, but an interesting one to me particularly because of the reorganization of the Texas Rangers as the Texas State Police. I found myself wondering how a former Ranger who still wanted to serve the state in law enforcement might react when he has to serve with such a corrupt unit, and thus I created Thorn Dawson. I found it difficult to write about his mission to infiltrate the outlaw gang without using the term *undercover*, a word that did not come into usage until the next century. I hope you enjoyed reading about his efforts to bring down the outlaw gang.

I would love to hear from you! You can write to me in care of Love Inspired Books, Harlequin, 195 Broadway, 24th floor, New York, NY 10007, or email me via my website at www.lauriekingery.com. Blessings,

Laurie Kingery

*With her uncle trying to claim her ranch, widow
Lula May Barlow has no time to worry about romance.
But can she resist Edmund McKay—the handsome
cowboy next door—when he helps her fight for her
land...and when her children start playing matchmaker?*

Read on for a sneak preview of
A FAMILY FOR THE RANCHER,
the heartwarming continuation of the series
LONE STAR COWBOY LEAGUE:
THE FOUNDING YEARS

"Just wanted to return your book."

Book?

Lula May saw her children slinking out of the barn,
guilty looks on their faces. So that's why they'd made such
nuisances of themselves out at the pasture. They'd wanted
her to send them off to play so they could take the book to
Edmund. And she knew exactly why. Those little rascals
were full-out matchmaking! Casting a look at Edmund,
she faced the inevitable, which wasn't really all that bad.
"Will you come in for coffee?"

He tilted his hat back to reveal his broad forehead, where
dark blond curls clustered and made him look younger
than his thirty-three years. "Coffee would be good."

Lula May led him in through the back door. To her
horror, Uncle sat at the kitchen table hungrily eyeing
the cake she'd made for Edmund...and almost forgotten
about. Now she'd have no excuse for not introducing them
before she figured out how to get rid of Floyd.

"Edmund, this is Floyd Jones." She forced herself to add,
"My uncle. Floyd, this is my neighbor, Edmund McKay."

As the children had noted last week when Edmund first

stepped into her kitchen, he took up a good portion of the room. Even Uncle seemed a bit unsettled by his presence. While the men chatted about the weather, however, Lula May could see the old wiliness and false charm creeping into Uncle's words and facial expressions. She recognized the old man's attempt to figure Edmund out so he could control him.

Pauline and Daniel worked at the sink, urgent whispers going back and forth. Why had they become so bold in their matchmaking? Was it possible they sensed the danger of Uncle's presence and wanted to lure Edmund over here to protect her? She wouldn't have any of that. She'd find a solution without any help from anybody, especially not her neighbor. Her only regret was that she hadn't been able to protect the children from realizing Uncle wasn't a good man. If she could have found a way to be nicer to him… No, that wasn't possible. Not when he'd come here for the distinct purpose of seizing everything she owned.

The men enjoyed their coffee and cake, after which Edmund suggested they take a walk around the property to build up an appetite for supper.

"We'd like to go for a walk with you, Mr. McKay," Pauline said. "May we, Mama?"

Lula May hesitated. Let them continue their matchmaking or make them spend time with Uncle? Neither option pleased her. When had she lost control of her household? About a week before Uncle arrived, that was when, the day when Edmund had walked into her kitchen and invited himself into her…or rather, her eldest son's life.

"You may go, but don't pester Mr. McKay." She gave the children a narrow-eyed look of warning.

Their innocent blinks did nothing to reassure her.

Don't miss
A FAMILY FOR THE RANCHER
by Louise M. Gouge, available August 2016 wherever
Love Inspired® Historical books and ebooks are sold.

Turn your love of reading into rewards you'll love with
Harlequin My Rewards

Love the Love Inspired book you just read?

Your opinion matters.

Review this book on your favorite book site, review site, blog or your own social media properties and share your opinion with other readers!